OLD BOB'S GIFT

OLD BOB'S GIFT

Life in the Catskill Mountains
of the 1850s

JEFF MUISE

ILLUSTRATED BY JOE TANTILLO

S H A W A N G U N K

The Shawangunk Press
Wappingers Falls, New York

Text and cover design by Joe Tantillo.
Illustrations copyright © 1996 by Joe Tantillo.

ISBN 1-885482-04-3

First printing, October 1996.

10 9 8 7 6 5 4 3 2 1

♻ Printed on acid-free, recycled paper.

Library of Congress Cataloging-in-Publication Data

Muise, Jeff, 1946–
    Old Bob's gift / Jeff Muise ; illustrated by Joe Tantillo.
        p.   cm.
    Summary: While working in a sawmill in the Catskill Mountains of New York in the 1850s, fourteen-year-old Matt not only learns craftsmanship but also valuable lessons about life.
    ISBN 1-885482-04-3 (pbk. : alk. paper)
    [1. Catskill Mountains Region (N.Y.)--Fiction. 2. New York (State)--Fiction. 3. Lumbermen--Fiction. 4. Bullies--Fiction.]
    I. Tantillo, Joe, ill. II. Title.
    PZ7.M884701 1996
    [Fic]—dc20
                                                                96-4929
                                                                CIP
                                                                AC

To my father, Robert K. Muise

A Barn
Raising

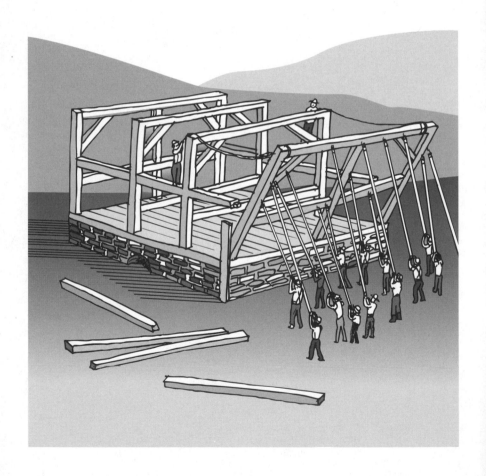

Contents

With their highest peaks barely topping 4,000 feet, the Catskill Mountains of New York State would not be listed among the most majestic mountains of the world. But the Catskills towered over the early history of New York and America.

What the Catskills lack in grandeur they more than make up for in picturesque charm. Sprawled on the west side of the Hudson River, these humped and jumbled mountains are cut through by streams tumbling down rocky falls under stands of hemlock and hardwood. The Catskills' romantic charm has captured hearts since the first Dutch settlers built their stone houses here in the 1600s.

In the early 1800s, the Catskills' beauty gained worldwide renown in the work of writers and artists. The Catskills were the setting for the story of Rip van Winkle, Washington Irving's timeless tale of the old Dutchman who fell asleep for twenty years. James Fenimore Cooper's fictional frontier hero Natty Bumppo hiked the mountains too and described their beauty in Cooper's *The Pioneers*.

But perhaps the most vivid depictions of the Catskills' charm were in paintings. The mountains' cascading falls, lakes, views, and cliffs were favorite subjects for the Romantic painter Thomas Cole and a host of other landscape artists of the Hudson River School in the early 1800s.

At the time of our story, in 1858, romance had given way

to practicality in the Catskills. Steep farms had taken over much of the Catskills' lower slopes and men harvested mountain forests for lumber and hemlock bark for leather tanning. Waterfalls were less admired for their natural beauty than for the power they could provide a sawmill or gristmill. It was a time of rural industry and farms.

Now, many people look back on those old days of barn raisings and husking bees as a simpler, better time. It was certainly simpler, but life then had its own set of hardships and challenges. Meet Matthew Quick, the hero of our story, and visit those bygone days in the Catskills to see what life was like for one boy.

Chapter One

Matthew Quick

The drowsy boy lay in the dark and listened to his grandmother move around in the kitchen below. He heard the iron lids of the wood-burning cookstove rattle as she tended the crackling fire within. Soon, he felt the heat from the stove rising into his loft bedroom in soft currents, mixing with the cold April air that had seeped in overnight through the slanted roof just over his head. Matthew Quick knew that in just a few minutes his grandmother would come to wake him. He closed his eyes and let his mind drift back to the thoughts with which he had fallen asleep—the thoughts of his life before. Matt slipped back into a dream, a dream in which his mother fried eggs in their old kitchen and his father sat at the kitchen table and sipped coffee from a tin cup. His father looked up at him and seemed to call his name, but the voice was not his father's.

"Matthew," the voice repeated. The dream dissolved as the gentle voice urged him awake, and in the candlelight at the foot of his bed Matt could just make out the face of his grandmother. "Wake up, Matt. It's time to get up. It'll be dawn soon, and you start work at the sawmill today."

"I'm gettin' up, Grandma," the boy mumbled and raised himself on his elbows.

"Breakfast will be ready soon," she said, lighting the candle by the boy's bed. "Don't tarry now." The old woman shuffled out the low door and Matt could hear the steep stairs creak as she climbed back down to the kitchen below. He yawned, stretched, and swung his legs to the wide board floor.

Matt hiked up his homespun wool pants, buttoned on a rough cotton shirt that had been his father's, and slung his green suspenders up over his shoulders. He stooped to lace his shoes, and as his fingers performed the familiar task, he thought about the day's work ahead.

At fourteen, work was nothing new to the farm boy. In 1858, there was plenty of work for everybody in these Catskill Mountain hinterlands: hay to cut, stone fences to stack, firewood to split, and water to carry. Farms meant hard work, and farms were everywhere. They nestled in hollows, draped over the round tops of hills, and clung to the mountainsides. Steep fields climbed nearly to the tops of many of the lower mountains before giving way to woods (the cows that grazed those upland pastures grew their legs longer on one side, the farmers joked), and everywhere the open and rumpled landscape was quilted with stone fences. Men had worked lifetimes on this quilt. They had begun as boys.

So had Matt. Since he was old enough to lift an armful of fresh-cut hay, Matt had helped with the haying in the summer. He had climbed Mombaccus Mountain to cut saplings for his father to shave into barrel hoops in the long winter months and sell to the cooper in Port Jackson. He had split firewood, gathered nuts, and spent a whole week one summer staining his fingers blue picking huckleberries on the scrub pine ridge above Ellenville.

But for Matt, working at the sawmill for money was different. As a young man, his father had worked at the sawmill too, and the work signified manhood to Matthew. The boy wondered if he could measure up to manhood.

Matt carried his candle over to a small table that held a shallow basin and a pitcher of water. He poured some water in the basin, then splashed it on his face and studied himself in the looking glass on the wall. In the candlelit mirror, he saw a slender boy with tousled brown hair, a high forehead, and ears that stuck out a little. Matt noticed that his brown eyes had a sadness to them that didn't used to be there. And he saw that his father's shirt was too big for him, even after his grandmother's alterations.

Matt clambered down the stairs to the kitchen below, where his grandmother was vigorously poking the fire in the cookstove, sending a dancing flame and a small stream of sparks aloft into the dimly lit room. When she had stirred the fire, she slid a black iron griddle over the hot spot on the stovetop and began to ladle thick dollops of pancake batter out of a bowl onto the hot griddle with a wooden spoon. The batter hissed as it hit the hot metal. At the right rear of the stovetop, a small pitcher of maple syrup warmed. It was new syrup, fresh from this spring's recent sap run. At the left rear of the stove, another pot containing a soup bone and an odd mix of vegetables bubbled lazily.

"There's a cup of milk on the table, Matt. And there's plenty more where that came from. Clara almost overflowed the bucket this morning," his grandmother said. She smiled at Matt and turned back to tend the pancakes.

Matt's grandmother's given name was Emily, and she was Matt's father's mother. She was a stout woman dressed in a light blue homespun dress with a collar that rose clear to her chin. She wore a red-checkered apron

3

with a big catch-all pocket in the front where she kept cooking implements, her spectacles, and even the odd egg she occasionally found, left by a wayward hen in a pile of hay or coil of rope. Emily Quick's hair was white and tied back, making her high forehead appear even higher. But there was nothing severe in her face, which always seemed about to smile—even when there was precious little to smile about.

"It should be a good clear day today. I saw the stars out when I went to milk the cow," Matt's grandmother said as she joined him at the table with the platter of pancakes.

Matt took a long drink of the thick, fresh milk, then licked away the white moustache it left clinging to his upper lip. The milk was still warm from the cow and tasted rich and good. Matt noticed he was hungry, and he dug into the stack of pancakes eagerly. Matt and his grandmother ate quietly for a time, with the only other sound the crackling of the woodfire in the cookstove.

In the flickering candlelight, Matt looked around at his new home. The cottage he shared with his grandmother was mostly one big kitchen. On one wall, it had an old stone fireplace with a black iron pot hanging in it. With the winter over, the fireplace was cold now. The cookstove was enough to heat the cottage. The kitchen had an iron sink under the window with a hand pump and a set of open shelves along one wall that held the dishes and cooking pots. Under the steps to the loft was a small door opening to stone steps down to the root cellar, and by the door were bins for potatoes, onions, and apples in their seasons. Overhead, fragrant herbs hung from the beams, drying. One corner of the room was dominated by the spinning wheel that Emily had worked on since she was a girl on her own parents' farm. She hadn't used it much for a few years, now that bolts of factory-made cloth were on sale in the stores. The room also had several straightback chairs and two rocking chairs, and there was a small room off the back where Emily slept on an old four-poster bed with a deep feather mattress. Upstairs, up under the eaves, was Matt's loft room and a small storeroom that held a couple of trunks for clothes, blankets, and such. As houses go, theirs was plain, but it was cozy and clean.

As Matt ate his breakfast, he thought back on the events of the past few sorrow-filled months. The series of tragedies that had changed his life had begun back in September. Matt still couldn't believe all that had happened in that short time.

The first blow had been the death of Matt's father, John, who was killed in a woodcutting accident. He was chopping down a dead tree for firewood—something he had done a thousand times since he was a boy. But this time, when the tree toppled, a rotten limb at the top snagged in another tree, broke off, and fell back in the opposite direction. Matt's father never knew what hit him—at least that's what the other woodsmen had said. It was a common sort of accident; the woodsmen even had a name for the rotten limbs at the tops of trees—"widow-makers," they called them.

But Matt's mother, Catherine, was a widow only a short time. After John Quick's death, she seemed to lose her vitality. She ate poorly, cried often, and in a matter of weeks had grown drawn and pale before Matt's eyes. Then his mother had gotten sick. The doctor said it was cholera. The epidemic that had killed dozens of people in the Rondout area had been over for almost three years, but cholera still stalked the countryside, and every year some people came down with it.

Matthew and his grandmother had tended his mother day and night, mopping her fevered brow or trickling water from a cloth between her dry lips. During the days she lay helpless, she often moaned John's name, and Matt's too. The boy was sick with worry and fear, but he tried to hold up bravely. At last, when his mother slipped away, he took comfort in the peace that seemed to claim her face. He had exhausted his bravery, and he cried until his tears were exhausted as well.

The final blow was the loss of the Quick family farm. Matt's grandfather, Noah, had started the farm almost forty years before. He had cleared the land from forest, stacked the first stone fences, planted the crops, and built a little cottage for himself, his new wife Emily, and their infant son, John. Later, as the farm prospered and grew, he had built a larger house for his family at another spot. When Noah had died a dozen years earlier, Matt's father had taken over the farm. Although Matt could not remember his grandfather, he felt as if he knew him from all the homesteading stories his grandmother had told around the supper table. In Matt's childhood, things had been good for the Quick family, and the boy had been happy.

Then the balance of fortune tilted the other way. There were some bad years for the crops—especially the drought in 1854 that baked the fields to dust. The weather was so parched that year the wells went dry, the streams all dwindled to trickles, and many acres of woodland burned in forest fires. Even the swamps and peat bogs dried up, and as the peat baked under the unrelenting sun, it mysteriously caught fire underground, invisibly burning the trees at their roots. Farmers spoke in amazement of seeing apparently healthy trees at the bog's edge suddenly topple and fall, as though felled by ghosts.

That year, the farmers all suffered, and everywhere money was tight. Matt's father had to go to the bank and take a loan on the farm to get the money the family needed to make ends meet. After that, besides the work on the farm, Matt's father had taken whatever odd jobs he could find to earn extra money to keep up with the loan payments—that last woodcutting job had been one of them.

After Matt's parents died, there was no way he and his grandmother could keep up the payments on the loan. First, there were threatening letters in the mail and then visits by the stern loan officer from the bank. Next, Matt recalled sadly, a legal notice had appeared in the *Kingston Democratic Journal:*

> *Mortgage Sale: Whereas John Quick, late of the Town of Rochester, in the County of Ulster (now deceased), on the twelfth day of October, A.D. eighteen hundred and fifty-four by a certain Indenture of Mortgage, executed by him, bearing the date, the day and the year aforesaid, given to secure the payment of . . .*

The legal notice went on for a full column in long sentences that Matt could not understand. The words meant the bank was taking the farm, his grandmother told him tearfully one night. The Quick farm would be sold to the highest bidder.

At last, one bleak winter afternoon, the farm was sold at auction. The bank took its mortgage money first, but there was a little left for Matt's grandmother, and luckily the farm's new owner had been willing to let her buy back the small plot of land that included the cottage where she had started out as a young wife with her husband, Noah. Now she was starting over again there with her grandson.

The unhappy string of events had all led up to this chilly April morning after a gloomy winter. Matt and his grandmother sat in the cottage and ate their breakfast in silence.

"This first-run syrup is sweet, isn't it?" his grandmother said at last.

Matt nodded. The earliest sap boiled down to the sweetest maple syrup. Matt had always looked on maple-sugaring time in March as the fresh start of a new year. Now it was the fresh start of a new life as well.

"I think I need to whittle some new sumac spiles for next year," Matt said. Spiles were the wooden spouts that were driven into holes in the maple trees to collect the sap. A sumac limb had a pithy center that was easy to hollow out and made good spiles.

His grandmother agreed, and soon the talk turned to a dozen other ordinary matters of country life: did Lucy the mare need reshoeing? Would there be any more snow? And the hand pump had been making a gasping sound lately—did Matt think it needed a new leather gasket? Matt was somehow cheered by the talk. It reminded him of the breakfast conversation with his family before.

When Matt had cleaned his plate, the time had come to

begin the three-mile walk to Samsonville. He put on his wool jacket with the big bone buttons, picked up his lunch pail, kissed his grandmother, and stepped out into the gray pre-dawn light. His grandmother stood in the open doorway hugging a worn woolen shawl around her shoulders.

"I know you'll do fine, Matt. Don't you worry none," his grandmother said. "And you give my best to Mr. Keator—and Mrs. Keator too, if you should see her."

Matt said he would, and he set out across the field toward the road. His feet made crunching noises as he walked over the churned frozen earth; Matt knew the field would go back to being muddy after the sun had hit it for a while. When Matt reached the dirt road, he turned to look back at the cottage and was surprised to see his grandmother still standing in the doorway. He waved once more, then directed his steps down the dirt road toward the hamlet of Samsonville.

Soon, Matthew had left the cottage behind, and Paltz Point, a stone knuckle on the distant Shawangunk Ridge to the east, had begun to be visible against a narrow band of peach-colored sky. Matt could see his breath in the cold morning air and could feel the cold pouring off the ground. He could still see patches of snow in the shaded depths of the woodlots he passed.

Matt's route led past their old house, and as he passed it, he could not stop his thoughts from returning to his mother and father. The memories made him sad, and he turned his eyes away only to see their familiar barn across the road. There was lantern light coming from the barn as the new owner tended to the livestock—just as Matt's father would have done at this hour of the day.

At last, Matt's gaze took refuge in the heavens and, to distract himself, the boy picked out and named the familiar constellations and stars his father had taught him—the dipper shape of the Big Bear, the vague horned shape that was Taurus the Bull, and the North Star that hung above the dark shape of Mombaccus Mountain. Some people said the future was foretold in the stars. Matt wondered what the heavens had in store for his grandmother and him.

Matt walked to the sawmill with his eyes fixed on the stars, until one by one they began to disappear into the larger light of the coming day.

Chapter Two

The Sawmill

The rays of the rising sun still had not reached the hollow where Samsonville lay when Matt crossed the bridge over rushing Mettacahonts Creek and turned up the narrow side road that led to George Keator's sawmill. Over his shoulder, Matt could hear the men talking downstream at the leather tannery. Even in the cold morning air, the pungent smell of the cowhides and the hemlock bark steeping in the tanning vats was so strong it pinched his nose. The story was that men working around those vats had their faces and hands tanned like leather by the rising vapors. Matt had seen those faces and they certainly looked leathery enough.

Mr. Keator's sawmill was located just upstream from the bridge next to a waterfall flowing out of an old millpond. The sawmill was not as important a business in Samsonville as the tannery was, but it held a kind of historical distinction. A mill of one sort or another had been at the waterfall for as long as anybody could remember. The waterfall had been a big reason a village had sprung up there in the first place.

It was a familiar pattern in the Catskill Mountains, where a waterfall often was the seed from which a village would sprout and grow. First, a sawmill would be built at a waterfall in the wilderness, to saw lumber from the abundant timber. Then, as the land was cleared and the timber used up, a gristmill would move in to grind flour from the wheat grown on the new fields. Soon, a store would open to sell goods to the farmers who brought their grain to the mill; then a blacksmith, a cooper, and others would add their trades to the growing hamlet. As time passed, roads from the surrounding countryside would wind their way to the spot, and eventually a settlement would bloom where once there had been only a waterfall.

In Samsonville's case, a tannery had opened in 1831, and since then the hamlet had grown steadily. Now it was a bustling village with a stable, a blacksmith shop, Tripp's General Store, Schoonmaker's Restaurant, Markle's Hotel for the tanners and other businesses. From dawn to dusk, the streets of the little boom town teemed with wagons loaded with cowhides or hemlock bark. Most of the people in the hamlet worked at the tannery, or sold something to the tannery, or sold something to the people who worked at the tannery. There wasn't much in the hamlet not connected to the tannery.

It was no surprise that when the village grew big enough to warrant a name, it took the name of its leading citizen and commercial benefactor, General Henry A. Samson, the principal partner of the tannery and a general in command of the Eighth Brigade of the New York State Militia. Finally, with the establishment of its own Dutch Reformed Church in 1851, Samsonville gained its full measure of respectability. Now Samsonville's name was printed in big letters on the map.

And at the waterfall that had started it all was Mr. Keator's sawmill. The sawmill was just a rustic frame structure supporting a tin roof to shelter the sawmill workers, the saw, and the machinery that moved the log carriage back and forth bearing the logs. Like everything else in Samsonville, Mr. Keator's sawmill was connected to the tannery, too. Its main business was to saw planks and timbers out of the hemlock trees chopped down and left behind by the bark peelers who supplied the tannery with bark. There was no large-scale commercial market for the hemlock lumber, but there was a steady demand for thick hemlock planks to keep up the plank roads that lately had been built in the Catskills and to build the huge icehouses that lined the Hudson River. The local farmers also used the hemlock lumber for barn framing, siding, fences, and a hundred other purposes.

There were more than enough logs to fill the sawmill's demand. The tannery's bark peelers worked much faster cutting down trees than the sawmill could saw planks. For every hemlock log sawed up by a Catskill Mountain sawmill, a hundred more rotted in the woods.

Now the sawing season was in full swing. It had been a snowy winter, and Mr. Keator was twice blessed. Thanks to the heavy covering of snow on the ground in January and February, it had been easier for the oxen teams to drag the logs out of the woods. As a result, the millyard was piled high with logs. Now, with the spring, that same snow was melting and had filled the millpond to the top of the dam. There was plenty of water to run the mill. As soon as there was enough light to work by, the water would be directed down the plank-built channel—the flume—to the millwheel. The sawyers, as the sawmill workers were called, would be making the most of the springtime high water. As long as there was daylight, they would be at work.

When Matt reached the millyard, he spotted Mr. Keator hunched over the big circular saw, and he turned his steps that way. As he walked through the yard, the boy inhaled the rich smell of the freshly cut wood and felt the thick, springy sawdust carpet underfoot.

"Hello, Mr. Keator," he called out.

"Well, good morning to you, Matt," Mr. Keator said. The sawyer stood up from the saw, which he had been sharpening with a metal file. Mr. Keator was a short thick man with a perpetually unshaven look about him. He had dark bushy eyebrows, a sharp nose, and wore a shabby felt hat with a crumpled brim. His clothes were stained with grease and woodsap, and a soiled rag dangled from his back pocket. But the most conspicuous thing about Mr. Keator was the ever-shifting mound in his cheek—a huge plug of chewing tobacco. Mr. Keator tossed a glance and a bolt of tobacco juice toward the rushing water of Mettacahonts Creek, then turned and grinned at Matt.

"The creek's running like a stampede of horses, Matt. I hope you're ready to hitch 'er up and make a dollar," the sawyer said jovially.

Mr. Keator turned back to the saw—his pride and joy— and gave the gleaming teeth a last swipe with the greasy rag from his pocket. Mr. Keator had been a friend of Matt's family for years, and Matt's father had worked for him as a young man, too. That was back in the days when the sawmill still used the old straight-bladed up-and-down saw, and Matt's father had told the boy stories of long afternoons watching the slow progress of the sawing (the saw only cut on the down stroke). Mr. Keator had once promised Matt's father that he'd give his son work when he was old enough. Matt really wasn't old enough yet, but circumstances had changed, and Mr. Keator knew the promise to his friend had come due.

"Well, let's get you started then, Matt. First off, how about you go over and give Tom a hand moving the sawing scraps out of the way. We worked late last night and didn't have a gasp left to haul 'em clear," Mr. Keator said.

The sawyer spit in the direction of a boy of about sixteen who was hefting the long slender log scraps onto his shoulder and toting them clear of the saw to make way for the new ones that soon would be piling up.

Matt recognized Tom Pierce from the one-room schoolhouse in Palentown they had both attended a few terms back. He could see the older boy had grown considerably since then. He was tall and strapping and his rolled-up sleeves revealed forearms as thick as a man's. Tom's blond hair was shaggy, and when he brushed it away from his face, Matt saw the boy wore a sullen expression.

Tom hadn't gone to the Palentown school long, Matt recalled. He had started school late and had been far behind the other children in Schoolmaster Terbush's class, even the much younger children. Cranky Mr. Terbush had lost patience with Tom easily, and some of the other children, following their schoolmaster's lead, had laughed behind their hands at Tom whenever he failed at a lesson. The laughter had stopped after Tom bloodied a nose or two, but it wasn't more than a couple of months before Tom stopped coming to school, and Matt had not seen Tom since then. He walked over and stuck out his hand.

"Hello, Tom, I'm Matt Quick. Maybe you remember me from the school," Matt said with a smile.

The older boy ignored the outstretched hand. "Let's work your arm, not your jaw," Tom grunted as he shouldered a stack of scraps. He turned his back and started off with the load.

Matt's smile faded at the rebuff, but he shrugged it off and set to work. He made a pile of scraps as big as Tom's, then found he could not shoulder the heavy load. After removing some of the wood, Matt barely managed to lift the lightened load to his shoulder. He staggered a few steps, then lost control of the long awkward bundle, and it fell to the ground with a loud clatter. Matt lightened the load again and at last dragged it to the scrap pile.

"I thought Old Man Keator was going to get me some help," Tom said gruffly as he watched Matt dump his load. "I can carry that much under one arm."

"Th-that's all I can lift," Matt stammered. "I'll try to make faster trips." He turned and hurried back for another load.

Soon, the boys had cleared a spot near the saw for the new sawing scraps to accumulate. Mr. Keator waved his arm and shouted to a man up at the millpond. The man lifted the gate, and instantly a stream of water raced down the flume to the millwheel. The mill shuddered as the millwheel kicked to life with a chorus of creaks and groans and a low, powerful rumbling. The millwheel turned slowly at first, then faster, until it was turning at a good clip. Mr. Keator worked a lever, and there was the metal sound of gears coming together. Now the mill's gears began to turn, translating the millwheel's slow rotations into the much faster revolutions of the saw. In a few moments, the gleaming teeth had blurred into invisibility as the saw picked up speed with a loud humming sound.

With more shouts from Mr. Keator, two men rolled a log into position on the log carriage and secured it with the sharp iron hooks called log dogs. The men worked well together, each seeming to know what was expected of him and what the other man would do. When they had dogged down the log, Mr. Keator waved them away, then worked another lever. The log carriage gave a shudder and began to inch forward on its rollers, steadily bearing the log toward the furiously whirling saw.

Matt was startled at the high whining sound—almost a scream—as the saw began to rip through the first log of the day. Sawdust filled the air, and as the first slab of wood parted from the log, the boys pulled it clear of the saw. After several more passes, the log had been sawed up into a dozen rough, bark-edged boards that Mr. Keator called flitches. Following Tom's lead, Matt helped stack the flitches back onto the log carriage so the sawyer could run them through the saw again to cut off the bark and make the finished square-edged planks. Then, while another log was set up on the log carriage, Matt and Tom hurried to stack the new planks, toss the leftover bark edges and slab wood onto the scrap pile, and get ready to do it all again with the next log. Soon the boys were working as fast as they could.

The work was as hard as Matt had expected and harder. Within a couple of hours, despite the cool air, he had hung his coat on a tree branch and was working in his shirt-sleeves. Matt was dripping with sweat and his face was coated with sawdust. His muscles ached, and he had a long painful splinter in the heel of his right hand. At last, Mr. Keator stopped the saw and ordered the flume gate closed.

Keator's Mill

Flitches

"You boys take a blow for a bit while I touch up the saw. That last knotty log took the edge right off it," Mr. Keator said.

Matt walked over and sat next to Tom under a leafless tree. He had not spoken to the boy since the earlier rebuff and tried again now to break the ice. "Well, Tom, what have you been doing since you left school? I haven't seen you around," Matt asked.

"I don't waste my time being talked at by a schoolmaster when there's a man's work to be done," Tom said. "Look what school's done for you. I've seen beanpoles bigger than the arms you've got." Tom's voice was thick with disdain.

Matt looked away in embarrassment. He could feel his ears grow hot, and he knew they were red. An uncomfortable moment passed as Matt tried to think of a way to respond to Tom's insult.

Suddenly, a merry voice carried over the roar of the creek. "Tommy! Tommy!"

Matt looked up to see a small curly-haired girl in a red cloak waving from a wagon at the edge of the millyard. He heard Tom shout a greeting, and he was struck by the change that had come over the surly boy.

"Hey, we got a mouse in the millyard!" Tom shouted as a broad smile claimed his face. "I guess I'd better roust it out."

Tom jumped to his feet. He sprinted over to the wagon, chased down the squealing child, and tossed her into the air again and again. It was a happy sight and, despite his earlier embarrassment, Matt couldn't help smiling as he watched the boy frolic with the little girl.

"That's Tom's mother and his little sister, Mary," said Mr. Keator, who had walked over and now stood at Matt's shoulder. The sawyer wiped his damp forehead with the rag from his pocket.

"Tom's somewhat partial to Mary, as you can see," Mr. Keator went on, "especially since he lost his other sister,

Sarah, to cholera two winters ago … but then I guess you know about cholera."

Mr. Keator fidgeted, then started to walk away, but he stopped and turned back to face the boy. Mr. Keator's jaw worked his plug of tobacco hard.

"I'm real sorry about your ma and pa, Matt. They were real fine people," the sawyer said in a somber voice. "It was a bad stroke, losing 'em both at once like that. May they both rest in peace."

Uncomfortable at the subject he had raised, Mr. Keator glanced away, and his eyes returned to the knotty log that had dulled his cherished saw.

"I guess life is full of knots sometimes too," the sawyer sighed. Mr. Keator fell silent as a long moment passed.

"Anyway, we're glad to have you working with us, Matt," he said, brightening. "We've got a good crew here. And don't you fret none about Tom. He's rough and moody, but he's all right when you get to know him."

The sawyer glanced skyward. "The sun's climbing like a scared coon. We'd better get cracking," he said. He gave a shout and waved his hand at a man by the flume gate. Soon the mill wheel rumbled to life again.

Matt watched as Tom swung his sister up onto the wagon seat and spoke briefly to his mother. As the wagon rattled off, Tom waved and then turned and headed back to the millyard. Matt rose, dusting off his bottom.

The men took their spots. Mr. Keator gave the signal, worked his lever, and another log advanced toward the saw. As the saw whined through the hemlock log, it sent a fresh shower of sawdust into the air, where it swirled in the shafts of sunlight that had at last reached Samsonville hollow. Matt grabbed the first flitch as it parted from the log and tossed it onto the growing pile.

Hours later, the western sky off toward Sundown had gone from deep red to purple as Matt trudged up the hill from Samsonville. The boy was bone tired; his shirt was stiff with dried sweat and sawdust, and his skin itched all over. Matt breathed a sign of relief when he cleared the last knoll and saw the candle in the window of the cottage across the field. Soon, he was sitting at the kitchen table hungrily spooning his grandmother's thick, steaming vegetable soup into his mouth. Matt was too tired to speak.

"How was your first day at the sawmill?" his grandmother finally asked. She slipped another chunk of wood into the cookstove and put an iron kettle of water on the stovetop to heat.

"Oh, the work's hard, but Pa didn't mind hard work, so I guess I don't either," Matt said. He spread butter on a thick slice of bread and used the bread to sop up the soup left in the bottom of the bowl. The good food made him feel better.

His grandmother nodded and turned to the cookstove to stir the fire. Springtime or not, the Catskill nights were still cold. Matt looked up from his eating and watched his grandmother. He thought he saw a little of his father in her high forehead and in a certain look in her eyes. He'd seen those same feature in his own looking glass too, and it somehow comforted him to see the family resemblance carried on.

Matt's grandmother wiped her hands on her apron. She walked over behind the seated boy and put her hand on his shoulder. "You'd better clean up now and get to bed.

You'll need your strength again tomorrow. The water in the kettle will be warm enough to wash in another minute," she said.

Matt nodded slowly. Bed sounded good to him, too.

"I got some dried apples up out of the cellar today. I'll sugar some and put them in your pail tomorrow," his grandmother added.

Soon, Matt had rinsed off the sawdust, dried himself, and crawled under the familiar patchwork quilt his mother had made. As he waited for sleep, he thought of his parents, remembering small things: the lock of hair that always hung in his father's face and the way his mother used to cock her head and wipe her hands on her apron when he spoke to her. He thought drowsily of the sawmill, and of Mr. Keator, and of Tom. Matt drifted into sleep, and his drowsy thought became a dream, a dream in which Tom, his face as big and brooding as a thunderhead, loomed over him.

Chapter Three

Tom

M att was thirsty. He licked his lips and felt the fine, tasteless grit of sawdust on his tongue. When he flexed his knuckles to relieve the soreness there, his fingers stuck together from the hemlock sap that coated them. The hair on his head was stiff and matted with a mixture of sap, sweat, sawdust, and bark chips. He had sawdust in his ears.

"Come on, schoolboy, get moving. The saw's getting ahead of you again!" shouted Tom from the scrap pile.

Matt groaned to himself, wrapped his arms around another awkward load of the hemlock scraps, and dragged it to the ever-growing pile at the edge of the millyard.

Matt had been at the sawmill for just a few weeks but it seemed like forever. Each day, he got to the sawmill at daybreak and went right to work. He shoveled sawdust or stacked the newly sawed planks to dry or loaded the wagon with lumber to be delivered. Sometimes, he did odd jobs or ran errands, such as feeding and watering the big millyard workhorse, Goliath, or clearing a branch that had snagged in the millwheel, or fetching a file or a can of grease from the tool shed.

But mostly Matt spent his day like this, coated in sawdust, working with Tom, hauling the sappy, splintery hemlock slabs into piles. The work was dirty, hard, boring, and—worst of all—endless. No matter how many armloads of scraps Matt toted away, there were always more pouring out of the saw right behind. Sometimes Matt and Tom would haul them in a wagon to the tannery to be burned in the wood-fired boilers, sometimes they'd burn them right there in the millyard, and sometimes a nearby farmer who wanted some easy kindling would come by for a wagon load. But still the bark-edged scraps piled up.

"If flitches was riches, we'd all be wearing top hats," Mr. Keator liked to joke, but Matt found it hard to laugh.

About midmorning each day, Mr. Keator would give the crew a short break while he sharpened his saw and greased the rollers on the log carriage. Matt always took the opportunity to have a drink of water and talk to the two older men in the sawmill crew. There was slow-talking Ned—tall and skinny as a scarecrow and dressed about as well—and Basil, who had a rude sense of humor and was missing two fingers off his left hand from a sawmill accident. Both men had worked for Mr. Keator for years. In fact, neither had ever done much of anything else.

"I guess you could say I've got my fingers in the lumber business," Basil boasted to Matt upon their first meeting, as he grinned and waggled the stumps of the missing fingers at him. Matt heard the joke a half dozen more times during that first week at the sawmill and he laughed along with Basil each time. Matt got along just fine with Ned and Basil.

But Matt made no headway with Tom, though he tried several times a day to get a conversation going with the older boy. Tom seemed to be on gruff terms with the older men, but he always turned a cold shoulder to Matt. When the two worked together on a chore, and Matt was uncertain about what was to be done or could not lift what was to be lifted, Tom was impatient and grumbled insults. Tom never used Matt's name. Whenever he had to address him, he called him "schoolboy" in a tone that suggested the term was an insult.

Matt could not understand what was behind Tom's unfriendly attitude. When he and Tom had been in school together three years earlier, Tom had been quiet and moody, but Matt had never had a run-in with him. These days, Tom seemed worse than moody, Matt thought. He seemed angry—angry at everything and angry at nothing.

Tom even worked with anger. Tom never just dropped an armload of sawing scraps—he threw them down violently. And when he used the ax, he attacked the log and sent off a shower of wood chips. Matt always felt uncomfortable around Tom and was afraid that he would say or do something wrong that would set him off.

But there was another side to Tom, the side that only emerged when his mother and his sister Mary stopped by the millyard. At those times, Tom showed a gentleness and kindness that Matt hardly believed could exist inside the same skin with the boy's angry side. Tom doted on his little sister, and it was obvious that she loved him with her whole heart, too.

As the days went by, Matt began to feel frustrated that, try as he might, he could not break through to Tom's better side.

"I don't know what it is, but it's almost like there's something about my being there that makes Tom mad," Matt confided to his grandmother one Saturday night as they talked after supper. "No matter what I say or do, he takes it wrong or finds an offense, and if I try to help him, he insults me."

Matt's grandmother was rocking in her favorite chair and knitting herself a shawl by the candlelight. She peered over her eyeglasses at Matt for a moment. All Matt could hear was her rocking chair creak and the knitting needles click. At last, Matt's grandmother cleared her throat and spoke.

"I know a story that might help you understand Tom a little better," she said.

Matt sat attentively and waited as his grandmother pursed her lips and chose her words. Emily was always slow to start a story, but once underway her stories had a rambling, headlong way about them, like a stone rolling down a hill, gathering speed.

"I guess you know that Tom's father, Cyrus Pierce, died three years ago," she began at last. "You may not know that your father and Cyrus were good friends as boys. Cyrus was as friendly a boy as you'd ever want to know, but he never had a taste for work or education or any of the disciplines a man has to learn. During school, he was elsewhere. At haying time, he'd show up with his scythe and cut a swathe as fast as anyone—but don't look away, because when you looked back, you'd see his scythe leaning up against a tree and Cyrus would be gone.

"By the time Cyrus got to manhood, he pretty much split his time between hunting and fishing. He just couldn't seem to settle down to work—even after he married Althea, and she'd had Tom. Oh, Cyrus would get a short-term job sometimes—like picking apples or ditching a field—but he was a poor worker and he'd never get another job from that same farmer. So it was mostly hunting and fishing for Cyrus—I do believe his family lived on rabbit stew in those days. But your father and he were still friends and they occasionally made a hunting or fishing trip together."

Matt's grandmother paused to draw a breath, and a sad look passed over her face. She rocked a little faster and went on.

"Then a terrible thing happened. Cyrus took up drinking rum. Althea tried to get him to stop drinking. She pleaded with him, and she had the Reverend McHarlow and the people from the Temperance Union out to the house to warn Cyrus off liquor. She even got your father to go down there one night to reason with Cyrus man to man, but I guess it turned into shouting, and John came home mad, and Cyrus kept right on drinking," she said.

"All this time, Tom was getting older. And whatever other faults Cyrus had, he loved his boy. Whenever he was sober, he and Tom would hunt and fish, and they were as close as a father and son could be. But meanwhile, because of the drinking, Cyrus was piling up debts and his reputation was gettin' shabbier and shabbier in the town."

Matt's grandmother stopped talking again, but judging by her frown and the increased pace of her rocking, Matt could see that she was getting to the nut of the story, something unpleasant she would just as soon not have to repeat. Emily was a God-fearing woman who hated to speak ill of anyone, especially the dead and departed. It was against her nature and distasteful to her. But there was something she wanted Matt to know. She plunged ahead, like someone hurrying by a dead skunk in the road.

"Well, late one night John was over at the Terwilligers' house helping out when their cow was calving. They heard a noise out by the chicken coop and went out there with a lantern, and ..."

Matt's grandmother stopped rocking suddenly and dropped her knitting to her lap.

"Now you must never tell Tom you know this story!" she said, leaning toward Matt and shaking her finger. "It would be cruel!"

"No, Grandma. I won't say anything," said Matt, now wide-eyed and burning up with curiosity.

Emily started up rocking hard again, and the knitting needles switched back and forth in her hands as she resumed the story.

"Well, there was Cyrus in the chicken coop. He was drunk on rum, and he'd wrung one chicken's neck and was about to do in another. He looked up and saw Mr. Terwilliger and your father, and he looked down at the dead chicken, and he went to pieces with shame. Cyrus fell right to his knees and cried like a baby. He begged Mr. Terwilliger and your father not to turn him in and said he only killed the chicken because he needed food for the family and promised to pay. But Mr. Terwilliger just said, 'Cyrus, you didn't even pay me yet for the eggs laid by the chicken you just killed,' and he called him 'no-account trash' and said he would have the law on him."

Matt's jaw dropped. Chicken thieves were the lowest kind of common criminal. "W-what did Pa do?" he stammered.

"Your father offered to pay for the chicken—which was Terwilliger's best layer, too—but Terwilliger wouldn't have none of it. He told your father it was his citizen's duty to stand up in town court and tell what he had seen," she said. "And your father allowed that Mr. Terwilliger was right, so that's what he did."

"So what happened to Cyrus?" Matt asked.

"The town justice went easy on Cyrus. Everybody knew Cyrus wasn't bad, just weak-willed. He had to work off his debt to Mr. Terwilliger. Of course, the matter ruined what little reputation Cyrus had left, and he couldn't get work cleaning stables after that. That made Cyrus even more mad, and he drank more than ever, and when he got drunk, he let the rum do his talking. He blamed all his hard luck on Mr. Terwilliger, the town justice, and your father. That finished any friendship he and your pa had left." She sighed.

"About a year after all this happened, the liquor finally killed Cyrus. That left Althea with Tom and her two daughters, Sarah and Mary, her youngest," she said. "Tom was just about your age then—a little younger even. Then two years ago, Sarah got cholera and died, and that hit Tom and his family pretty hard, too. Tom just cherished that girl."

Matt's grandmother set down her knitting, and her rocking slowed to a stop.

"There's one more thing about Tom. The way I heard it, it was his own idea to go to school, and he had to defy his father to do it," she said. "It was something of a sore spot between them. Cyrus never had gone to school, and he was against it—he called it 'putting on airs.' That was the reason Tom never went to school when he was younger. His father wouldn't allow it.

"Just think, Matt," his grandmother continued. "Tom

had to learn from his own father's bad example that a man needed education and hard work to amount to anything. It must have been a hard way for Tom to learn that lesson. Of course, when Cyrus died, Tom had no choice but to quit school and go to work."

Matt's grandmother smoothed out the shawl in her lap. "Well, that's about the whole of it—all I know, anyway," she said.

Matt was silent. He was thinking about his grandmother's story. He hadn't known about all the hard luck Tom and his family had had. It did help some things make sense—like Tom's quitting school—but he still didn't see why Tom would have it in for him. When his grandmother spoke again, it was as though she had read the question in his eyes.

"Matt, the way Tom's acting toward you might not be right or fair, but you can see why Tom might be angry because of the way things have turned out for him," his grandmother said. "He might even hold a grudge against our family—against you."

Matt frowned. He wondered how a notion like that might seem reasonable to somebody like Tom, yet be so dead wrong. He'd never done anything to Tom. He only wanted to get along with him.

"That doesn't make any sense, Grandma. I loved my father and mother too, but I don't hold a grudge against the world for allowing accidents in the woods or the cholera," he said.

By now Matt's grandmother had tucked her knitting away in the yarn bag. It was almost time for bed. She put her arms around Matt and hugged him.

"Matt, people have a lot of reasons for the way they are, and some are straight and clear, and some are muddled, and we can't do much about it either way. All you can do with Tom is be fair, be kind, and be yourself. Do it long enough and, sooner or later, he'll come around to the truth of it," his grandmother said.

The old woman picked up her candle and used it to light Matt's bedtime candle. She yawned and walked to the door of her bedroom, then turned and spoke again.

"You know tomorrow's Sunday, Matt. After church, if the weather is clear, what do you say we go out to the cemetery in Palentown and tend to John and Catherine's spot? We can put in those marigolds I started—it's getting warm enough—and we can take a picnic basket and a blanket and have a little visit with them—and with your grandfather, too," his grandmother said.

Matt and his grandmother had not been out to the graves since Easter, and that visit had been cut short by a cold, sleety rain. The trees had been bare then, and the wind had howled off Mombaccus Mountain. Now, the high tops of the mountains were still a drab gray, but in the lower-lying farm country, the grass had turned a vibrant green and the fields were splashed with flowers—violets and phlox and lily of the valley—more flowers than Matt could name. In the past week, the trees around their house had sprouted their first pale green and tender leaves. At the cemetery, Matt knew, the purple and white lilac blossoms would be bursting out soon—some might already be out. Matt realized that, almost beneath his notice, the Catskill landscape had been coming to life all around him.

31

The boy smiled and nodded at his grandmother. He kissed her on the cheek, took the candlestick from her hand, and climbed the narrow stairs to the loft and his bed under the eaves. Matt lay in the dark and thought about his grandmother's story until he fell asleep.

Chapter Four

A Visit to the Cemetery

Matt stood in the doorway of the cottage with the box of marigolds and felt the warmth of the sun wash over him. There was a sweet, fresh scent of flowers in the air and the songs of many birds. The boy put the box of flowers down on the bluestone well cover and worked the pump handle. As the clear water gushed out, it caught a ray of sunlight, and both water and light splashed at Matt's feet.

As Matt watered the marigolds, he marveled at how bright and sparkling the world was this day.

In the kitchen, Matt heard his grandmother humming to herself as she packed a basket with bread, slices of smoked ham and cheese, and a jar of blackberry jam, opened especially for the occasion. She folded a red checkered tablecloth, tucked it in the basket, and stood back to look with satisfaction at the picnic preparations. The sunny day and the good food in the bright basket were enough to please Emily.

Matt placed a gardening trowel and a watering can in the back of the wagon. He loaded the box of marigolds that his grandmother had sprouted on the windowsill of the cottage. Finally, he fetched the mare, Lucy, from their small barn and hitched her to the wagon. Now, everything was ready for the trip to the church in Samsonville. Matt stuck his head in the cottage door.

"Come on, Grandma," the boy called.

"I'll be there in a moment, Matt. I'm fixing my bonnet," his grandmother said.

Matt climbed up on the wagon and dusted off the seat with a handkerchief so he and his grandmother would stay clean for church. Matt's Sunday outfit was a neat pair of pants and a shirt. He didn't own a jacket like a few of the other boys in the village, but he wore his best suspenders, a black tie, and a straw hat that was nearly new. Emily had had a harder time deciding what to wear. She wanted a dress that was good enough for church, but not one too good to wear when she dug in the moist dark earth to plant the flowers at the cemetery. She settled for an old green print dress that had been set aside in the trunk for scraps. Fortunately, she had not had occasion to cut it up yet. She had shaken it out and pressed it with the flat iron heated on the cookstove. When she was done, the dress looked presentable, and she improved the outfit with a lace shawl and a bright white bonnet.

When his grandmother was ready, Matt helped her onto the wagon seat. Lucy was not a fast stepper, but the trip to Samsonville seemed to go quickly as Matt and his grandmother talked about the garden they would soon be planting and watched the spring scenery rolling by.

In the village, everybody was out and about, and the Dutch Reformed Church was even more crowded than usual. As a rule, Matt didn't mind church, but this time he thought Reverend McHarlow would never end his sermon. It had begun as a celebration of nature's rebirth in springtime; then it became a lecture on the necessary virtues of the countryman. Now the reverend's sermon was finishing up—as all his sermons seemed to do—with a warning against the sins of intemperance and dissolute living. Matt knew what intemperance was—drinking too much rum. He was a little vague about the nature of dissolute living.

At last Reverend McHarlow was done, and the congregation all filed out of the church into the sunshine. Many of the families went to the nearby church hall for the noon meal and a chance to socialize and exchange news with their neighbors. Sunday, after church, was often the only time that many of the people from around Samsonville saw each other. Matt and his grandmother usually joined the socializing too, but on this particular morning they had other plans.

Matt brought the wagon up to the low bluestone steps where the ladies could climb on, and his grandmother took her seat next to him. The boy flicked the reins and Lucy dutifully stepped off. As they headed out of town, up the steep hill from Samsonville, Matt let Lucy take the grade at her own pace.

The Palentown Cemetery was nearly on the way home—just a short side trip up Palentown Road. The cemetery was just off the road on a tree-shaded knoll that faced northward with a view of open fields and mountains. On the other side of the cemetery there was a woodlot with a small stream cutting through it. Matt turned the wagon up the dirt lane into the cemetery. When they reached a place where the grass was lush and thick, he tugged on the reins and Lucy stopped. Matt set the brake and climbed down from the wagon. He took the bit out of Lucy's mouth, so she could graze as she waited. He noticed there were several other wagons already there.

Matt gathered the tools and headed up the knoll to the

spot where his parents' graves were. His grandmother had already gone on ahead with the picnic basket. When he got there, he found his grandmother kneeling and praying at the gravestones. Matt stood behind her with his hand on her shoulder and read the brief inscriptions on his parents' stones:

John N. Quick

Died September 28, 1857

Aged 39 Years, 10 Months, 11 Days

and

Catherine, His Wife

Died November 12, 1857

Aged 37 Years, 4 Months, and 22 Days

There were three stones in all—Matt's grandfather's grave was there, too. All three stones were simple and square, but they stood straight and were well placed in the shade of several small white birch trees. Best of all, the plot had a wonderful view of Mombaccus Mountain.

Matt knelt beside his grandmother and offered up a prayer himself. He felt sad at the gravesites, and his eyes filled with tears. But Matt thought how he always felt much more sadness when he was at a place that was full of memories of his parents when they were alive. He still could not walk by their old house without feeling grief. And the other day he had broken down crying when his path led him through the blossom-laden old apple orchard and he recalled the cool fall afternoon when he climbed a tree to toss apples down to his mother. He remembered her bright upturned face and her laugh as she caught the apples in her apron, one by one. Those familiar places were everywhere, and Matt felt sadness every day. He only wished he could save all his sadness for the cemetery.

When he and his grandmother had finished their prayers, she smiled at Matt and dabbed at her eyes with a handkerchief. Matt took her hand and squeezed it.

"Let's put these flowers in, Grandma," the boy said softly, and the two set about the small task. Matt began by turning over the top layer of soil with the trowel while his grandmother gently worked the marigolds loose from the box. Then she carefully tucked them into the earth. As his grandmother planted, Matt went off to the adjoining woodlot to gather some smooth stones to line the edges of the graves.

Walking through the cemetery, Matt noticed little groups of solemn people gathered around other graves. In one group, he recognized Tom, his sister Mary, and their mother at the graves of Tom's father Cyrus and his sister Sarah. Tom and his mother, dressed in their Sunday best, had their heads bowed and their hands clasped in prayer. Little Mary, in a yellow calico frock, had her hands clasped reverently too, and Matt could see the girl look up into the face of her brother and then try to copy the sad expression she saw there. But staying quiet and prayerful for long seemed all but beyond Mary's childish powers of self-control. The little girl squirmed and her head swiveled this way or that with every rustle of the trees or distant bird song.

Suddenly, a golden butterfly fluttered past the Pierce family, and its bright beauty proved too much for Mary to bear. With a squeal, the little girl bolted after the butterfly and gave chase. Mary's yellow curls bounced wildly as she pursued the fluttering insect through the trees and groups of somber people. When the butterfly alighted on a bush and slowly fanned its wings, Mary tiptoed near, then made a sudden grab for the butterfly. The little girl squealed with frustration as the butterfly took off just ahead of her eager grasp.

The sight and sound of Mary's chase drew the attention of the other families at the cemetery, and many heads turned to follow the antics of the little blonde girl in the yellow calico dress as she scampered amid the gravestones. Finally, when Mary made a desperate lunge at the butterfly and tumbled harmlessly into a bush, the rippling sound of laughter dispelled the sadness at the Palentown Cemetery. Mary's small show was over, but smiles had replaced the grief on many a face, and the whole mood of the scene had changed. The cemetery's heavy silence was gone for that day, replaced by the happy sounds of a picnic as blankets and baskets were spread out among the gravestones.

Matt smiled to himself too as he wandered off to continue his search for smooth stones. Soon, he had gathered up an armful of stones and he started back. When he got closer, he was surprised to find that Tom, Mary, and their mother were sitting on the edge of the checkered tablecloth that his grandmother had spread out. His grandmother and Mrs. Pierce were talking, and Mary was licking blackberry jam off a piece of bread his grandmother had given her. Tom sat silently at the edge of the group. Matt's grandmother looked up as Matt approached.

"Matt, you know Mrs. Pierce and her daughter Mary,

don't you? Of course, you know Tom," his grandmother said brightly. "I invited them to join us."

Matt dumped his load of stones, smiled, and touched the brim of his hat. Althea Pierce smiled back, but Mary was too absorbed in her jam to notice Matt's arrival. Tom greeted Matt with a grunt.

Matt sat down on the grass, broke off a piece of bread, and chewed it slowly as he listened to his grandmother and Mrs. Pierce pick up the thread of their conversation. Matt had not seen Tom's mother close-up before. Now he saw that she was a thin woman with a look of constant worry around her eyes. Her brown hair, tied back haphazardly, was wiry and streaked with gray, and she unconsciously twisted the corner of a handkerchief as she spoke.

"Oh, things aren't too bad for us, Emily. I take in washing and mending, and Tom has his job at the sawmill, so we get along," Mrs. Pierce said. "Tom's a big help to me. On most Sundays, I do wash for the Samsons and Tom helps me by hanging the clothes out on the line."

Tom threw his mother a look, but she didn't notice and kept on talking.

"Why, he's become quite a good cook, too. He makes supper a couple of times a week if I'm too busy or tired. You should see how sweet he looks with the apron on," Mrs. Pierce said. Her hand fluttered to her mouth to cover a laugh as she glanced over at Tom with a loving look. The boy smiled weakly and squirmed inside his clothes, as though his shirt had suddenly become too tight.

"We're both lucky to have our young men around, aren't we?" Matt's grandmother said. She put an arm around Matt's shoulder and squeezed him affectionately, and it was his turn to feel uncomfortable.

By this time, Mary had cleaned the jam from the surface of the bread. She tossed the bread to a curious squirrel and scampered off to pick wildflowers at the edge of the neighboring field. The sunlight made Mary's curly hair glow as she skipped from one patch of blossoms to another. The girl studied and sniffed each flower before she gleefully added it to her growing collection. Mary was pretty—that much was obvious to anyone—but Matt could see it was her spirit that really set her apart. Mary could see only goodness and beauty in the world, and she reflected that delight back to those around her. It was no wonder Tom loved her so dearly.

When Mary had gathered her bouquet of flowers, she dashed back to the group. First, she thrust her face into the bunch to smell the blossoms, and then she made Tom do the same. He grudgingly sniffed. Tom's discomfort seemed to suggest mischief to his little sister. Her eyes sparkled as she began taking the flowers, one by one, and threading them into Tom's shaggy mop of hair.

"Don't do that," Tom said, and he gave his head a little shake, but the girl just giggled. Tom made a grab for the bouquet of flowers, but Mary dodged his hand and danced around behind him where he couldn't reach. The little girl laughed and Matt thought the laugh had a bit of the devil in it.

"Tom so pretty!" Mary said as she filled Tom's hair with the blossoms.

Tom's face was beginning to turn red now, and he cast an uncomfortable sidelong glance at Matt. When he saw

Matt grinning, Tom's lips compressed into a frown.

"Stop it, Mary!" he said again, but the girl would not take her brother seriously. She just laughed as she continued to poke the flowers into his hair.

Matt saw Tom's embarrassment and thought it might be easier on the boy if he weren't there.

"Grandma, I'm going over to the stream to fill the watering can. I'll be right back," Matt said. His grandmother smiled and nodded as she continued talking to Mrs. Pierce.

Matt picked up the watering can and headed over toward the brook. As he walked though the cemetery with the vivid image of Mary still fresh in his mind, Matt passed the grave of Tom's sister Sarah. He paused there a moment, thinking of Tom's loss, and as he went on he began to notice other small gravestones here and there. In many family plots, one or two or more of the stones were placed in memory of children who had died as infants, in tragic accidents, or, most often, as victims of the diseases that swept through the countryside from time to time. Cholera, scarlet fever, pneumonia, diphtheria, consumption, and smallpox were all common. Sadly, the doctors had cures for none of them.

Suddenly, Matt's thoughts were interrupted by the sound of laughter from back the way he had come. He looked up to see Mary at her sister's grave. The girl had once again caught sight of the golden butterfly and her renewed chase had brought her to the spot. As Matt watched, Mary climbed up onto her sister's gravestone to reach the butterfly, which had perched on a bursting lilac blossom that overhung the grave. Mary's eyes shone as she teetered on top of the gravestone and reached for the elusive beauty just beyond her grasp.

"Mary, come back here," Matt heard a voice call. Looking through the trees beyond the girl, he could see Tom coming at a trot.

The little girl did not hear her brother. Even her breathing had stopped as she concentrated on the object of her desire. Standing on tiptoe atop the gravestone, Mary stretched closer—the butterfly was almost within reach! The little girl made a sudden grab, and her look of expectation turned to surprise as she missed her mark and lost her footing. Mary waved her arms as she fought to regain her balance, but at last, with a little cry, she fell backward onto the soft grass covering her sister's grave.

As Tom ran up, a new mischief took shape in the little girl's mind. Mary clamped her eyes shut, crossed her arms above her chest, and lay quiet and still where she had fallen. Tom bent over to pick her up, and as he did the flowers dislodged from his hair and rained down on the girl's body. Matt saw Tom's face turn white at the sight of Mary's small, still form lying on the grave, covered with the flower petals.

"Look, Tom. Mary dead," the little girl said. Her lips twitched as she tried to keep from smiling.

The blossoms scattered as Tom seized his sister by the shoulders and jerked her roughly to her feet.

"No! You're not dead! You're not," Tom blurted. "Don't say that!"

Mary looked shocked. She stared at her brother, wide-eyed, and her lower lip began to tremble. Tom lifted his sister and hugged her. The boy had his eyes closed tight, and when he opened them Matt saw they were blurred with tears.

Tom had not noticed Matt until now. When their eyes met, Tom's expression hardened, and he turned away. Tom put his sister down, brushed off her yellow dress, and gently wiped away a tear that trailed down her cheek. Matt watched as Tom took Mary by the hand and led her away through the shadows and gravestones toward the brightness that marked the edge of the field.

Chapter Five

Matt Meets a Challenge

M att leaned on his shovel in the sawdust pile and listened to the early morning calls of the birds and the babbling of the brook. These sounds always seemed louder and clearer to him at this early hour. There was a sharpness to the air that seemed to carry the sound better—or maybe it was because the mill and nearby village were quieter then.

Whatever the reason, Matt liked the clear sounds of the morning, and he closed his eyes and opened his ears to it all: the babbling brook, the singing birds, Tom whistling …

… Tom whistling?

Had Matt heard right? He perked up his ears to be sure it was true. Yes, it was. Tom was whistling. He wasn't whistling loudly or well, but he was very definitely whistling. In all the weeks they had worked side by side, Matt had never heard Tom whistle before.

Thinking back, Matt realized there had been something else that was odd. When Matt had arrived at the sawmill, Tom had greeted him. The greeting was just a grunt and a "Mornin,' schoolboy," but for the first time the snarl had been missing from Tom's voice.

First the greeting, now the whistling. Something was up with Tom. Matt thought about asking what it was, but that might just invite trouble. Instead, he decided to wait and see what happened as the day went along.

Mr. Keator wasn't to be seen. Basil had said he was down

at the tannery talking to General Samson about some business and probably wouldn't be back for a couple of hours. Instead of sawing, the sawmill crew worked at other chores. Basil and Ned were off by the millpond making a minor repair to the flume, and Matt was busy filling the wooden wheelbarrow with sawdust and dumping it in the low spot in the woods just outside the millyard. He had just dumped a load and was spreading it out with his shovel when he looked up and saw Tom standing there. Matt was amazed to see that the boy was actually smiling now.

"Hey, schoolboy, get up out of the sawdust and help me get some of these logs rolled onto the skids," Tom said.

Matt leaned the shovel against the wheelbarrow and followed Tom over to where the unsawed logs were piled near the skids, which was what they called the ramp made of log rails leading to the log carriage. Once on the skids, the logs could be rolled easily down the slight incline to the log carriage, but first the logs had to be maneuvered to the top of the skids. It was a heavy job that Ned or Basil usually accomplished with the help of the horse, Goliath.

"Where's Goliath?" Matt asked.

"Oh, he must have picked up a pebble in his shoe," Tom replied. "He was a little gimpy this morning when I went to fetch him. I couldn't find the pebble, so I left him in the stall. He'll probably paw at the ground until he works the pebble out himself.

"Anyway, we can handle this job without no horse," Tom said. "Here—catch the cant hook."

Tom tossed the heavy tool to Matt, who caught it awkwardly. The cant hook was a heavy wood-and-steel tool the men used to handle the logs. It had a four-foot oak handle and, about a foot up from the end, a band of steel around it, from which swung a curved piece of steel with a hooked point. The idea was to sink the hook into a log—then you could put your shoulder to the stout wood handle and use it like a lever to roll the log.

Matt looked at the logs waiting to be rolled to the skids. The line of logs began a good ten or twelve steps away from the top of the ramp.

"I'm bigger than you, so I'll take the butt end of the log," Tom offered. "You can take the poley end."

Matt looked at his end of the log. It was smaller than Tom's, but it was a long way from looking like a pole. Matt stepped up and got a grip on the log with his cant hook. On Tom's count, the boys put their shoulders to the handles and heaved. The log barely budged as Matt strained.

"Come on, schoolboy! Put some beef into it!" Tom said. "Again … on the count of three."

Once again, Matt put his full weight against the cant hook. The log slowly rolled a few inches forward.

Cant Hook

"All right. Let's take another bite and try again," Tom ordered. "We've still got a long way to go."

Matt shifted his cant hook again, and again strained against the handle on Tom's order. The log inched forward again. They repeated the operation twice more, and when Matt looked up he could see they were still more than ten feet from the top of the log ramp.

"And what might you two boys be up to?" a voice interrupted.

It was Basil, who had returned from repairing the mill flume. The man squinted at the boys as he tamped his corncob pipe with the stump of one of his missing fingers. "Why aren't you using the horse?"

Tom looked up at Basil and told him the story about the pebble in Goliath's shoe. Matt did not see Tom's sly grin or the wink he threw Basil as he spoke. Basil gave a little half-smile himself and struck a match against the heel of his boot.

"I'd give you young 'uns a hand, but we only have but two cant hooks," Basil apologized. He sucked on the pipe as he watched the boys work.

"That's all right, Basil. We can do it—right, schoolboy?" Tom said.

Matt nodded dumbly.

Again Tom counted, and again Matt threw himself heavily against the cant hook. The log had just begun to roll forward when the hook tore loose from the wood and Matt sprawled forward. His forearm raked across the rough log surface, leaving behind an angry red scrape and a trickle of blood. Matt pressed his hand against his wounded flesh and winced. He could feel his own salty sweat burning in the shallow wound.

"Hey—you lost it on us that time, schoolboy! Let's have at it again now," Tom said.

Basil frowned through the smoke curling out of his pipe,

then turned on his heel and walked away. Matt rubbed the pain from his arm, gamely reset the cant hook, and again put his shoulder to the tool to wait for Tom's count. He doubted he could move the log another inch, but he had to try if this was what it took to prove himself to Tom and the others.

"One, two ...," Tom began.

"Whoa, boys," said a man's voice.

There stood Basil, puffing on his pipe, his hand hooked in Goliath's bridle. "Well, boys, we're in luck. It looks like old Goliath kicked that pesky pebble loose and is set to go to work."

Goliath gave a little whinny and jerked his head up in a movement that looked like a nod. Matt laughed and turned to look at Tom. He was surprised to see the bigger boy wasn't smiling.

"You boys go back to the scrap pile. Goliath and I will pick up from here," Basil said.

The boys returned to their usual tasks and were at work only a few minutes when Matt saw Mr. Keator walk up the lane from the tannery. The sawyer called out for Ned and Basil to join him over by the log skids. Then he unrolled what looked to be a map and pointed at it as he held a conference with the two men.

For some reason, Tom was smiling again.

"Well, schoolboy, it looks like you'll be totin' slab wood by yourself for the next couple of days," Tom said. "Basil told me this morning that Mr. Keator was dickering to buy some timber out toward Sundown where the bark peelers are working—that's why he's been down at the tannery all day talking to General Samson.

"Means he'll be going out to the woods to have a look at it pretty soon, and, like always, he'll be needing a hand with him," Tom continued. "That's me. Mr. Keator calls it 'grading timber,' but it's just a camping trip to me. Heck, I might even be able to get in some fishin'," Tom said. The older boy grinned at the thought of cool mountain pools and jumping trout.

So that was the source of Tom's good humor! Matt recalled what his grandmother had said about Tom's love of hunting and fishing, and he grinned back. Tom started whistling again and was still whistling an hour later when Mr. Keator walked up.

"Listen, boys, I got another job for you. Come with me over to the wagon," Mr. Keator said. The boys dropped the wood scraps and followed the sawyer over to where the wagon sat, next to the supply shed.

"I promised I'd bring a couple of barrels of grease down to the tannery today," Mr. Keator said. "I want you two to hitch Goliath up to the wagon while I go shout up Ned and Basil to help us load these barrels on—they're as heavy as a loaf of my missus's bread." The sawyer, chuckling at his own joke, walked off down the lane.

Matt fetched Goliath and waited for Tom to help him hitch the horse up to the wagon. But instead of helping with the harness, Tom stood over the two short, squat barrels of grease. He looked over at Matt with a smile, but it was a hard sort of smile.

"I guess you thought those logs were pretty heavy this morning, didn't you, schoolboy?" Tom said. "Well, it's time you started getting used to heavy lifting if you're going to work with men and do your fair share."

Tom had rolled up his sleeves as he spoke, and now he walked up to the nearest barrel. The boy took a deep breath, stooped, and wrapped his arms around the middle of the barrel. He paused for a moment, then with a grunt and a heave, lifted the barrel clear off the ground. The veins in Tom's arms bulged and his face turned red as he stood straight up. He swung the heavy barrel onto the bed of the wagon, let it go with a thud, and the wagon sank on its springs under the weight. Tom casually dusted off his hands and turned to face Matt.

"I'll let you get the other one, schoolboy," Tom said. He grinned at Matt, but his eyes were narrow.

Matt looked hopelessly at the barrel. It looked as stout as a tree trunk. "Like a tree trunk," Matt thought to himself, and he grinned as the image in his mind became an idea.

Matt went into action. First, he leaned a couple of thick hemlock planks from the ground to the wagon bed to make a ramp. Then he fetched a coil of rope. Matt tied both ends of the rope up under the wagon seat and stretched the long loop down the ramp and out behind the wagon. Tom eyed Matt curiously as the boy pushed the heavy barrel on its side and rolled it onto the rope at the foot of the ramp. Matt brought the loop up over the barrel and tied it securely to Goliath's horse collar. Everything was set. Matt stood at Goliath's head and stroked the horse's thick neck.

"Easy, boy. Come on now. There's an apple in this for you," Matt coaxed Goliath. He showed the giant horse the apple he had brought for his noon meal.

Goliath whinnied and stepped forward. The rope tightened around the middle of the barrel and, as the horse continued forward, the barrel began to roll slowly up the plank ramp.

"Steady ... that's it," Matt whispered. Goliath moved forward slowly and the barrel steadily advanced up the plank ramp until it finally reached the wagon bed with a thump. Matt grinned to himself as he recalled watching his father use ramps and ropes in this same way to load heavy logs onto a logging sled.

"Attaboy, Goliath," Matt said. He stroked the horse's neck and offered the promised apple, then he looked over at Tom, expecting to see a sign of approval. Instead, the bigger boy just stood there with his arms folded across his chest. He was scowling and not saying a word.

Suddenly, there was the sound of a loud guffaw, and Matt and Tom turned to see Mr. Keator, Ned, and Basil watching from just down the lane. The sawyer stood with his hands on his hips and a look of amusement on his face. He shook his head and turned to the men. "Basil, Ned, maybe I don't need you boys after all. I've always said an ounce of brain is worth a hundred pounds of brawn and Matt's proved it again," Mr. Keator said. The men laughed, and Matt blushed at the praise.

Mr. Keator turned back to Matt and spoke again, this time in a more business-like tone.

"Say, Matt, that reminds me. I've got to go out in the woods over toward Sundown for a couple of days to look over some timber," Mr. Keator began."I'll need somebody good with arithmetic to help me reckon how much lumber there is, to calculate the board-feet and such. You've got some schooling. I'd like you to come along."

Matt felt the blush leave his face, replaced by a look of surprise. He stared at Mr. Keator. "B-but what about Tom? I thought ..." the boy began.

"Nah. If you come, I can leave Tom here to help with sawing. He's a good worker and that way we won't fall behind on our orders," Mr. Keator said. The sawyer had turned to direct this last comment to Tom and was surprised to find the boy wasn't in sight. Mr. Keator craned his neck this way and that, scratched his head, and spit a bolt of tobacco juice into the sawdust.

"Now where the devil has that boy gone to?" Mr. Keator said.

Chapter Six

At the Tannery

Tom's muttering could not be heard over his loud banging as he nailed a patch over the leaky spot on the sawmill's old tin roof. When he missed the nail and hit his thumb, the muttering erupted into a loud oath that brought Mr. Keator running out of the sawmill.

"Blazes, Tom! Mind your mouth! The women'll hear you down at the church hall!" the sawyer said angrily. "And take it easy up there! You'll be pounding more leaks into the roof than you're fixing!"

The sawyer shook his head and stalked back into the sawmill. Tom grumbled and went back to his task, banging as loudly as ever.

Matt knew why Tom was banging on the roof. He was angry about not getting to go on the trip to the hemlock woods. Matt was sure Tom blamed him, so he was keeping out of the bigger boy's way. With Tom on the roof, Matt had the scrap pile all to himself, which was fine. Matt kept remembering what his mother used to say: "Always give way to a bear in a berry patch." Matt guessed the advice applied to bears in millyards, too.

Matt was still working by himself hauling the slab wood scraps late in the day when Mr. Keator came by.

"Say, Matt, I've got to meet with General Samson at the tannery to go over some last details of this timber deal. I thought you might like to come along," he said.

Matt nodded quickly and dropped his load of wood

where he stood. He followed Mr. Keator down the lane toward the tannery site. As they neared the tannery, Matt was struck again by the overpowering smell of the place. The late May days were occasionally hot now, and the tannery was rank with the smell of the raw, untanned hides sitting in the sun amid clouds of flies. With the added smell of the tanning vats, Matt wondered how any man could stand to work here. He wrinkled his nose and considered that maybe he should have stayed back at the sawmill after all, even with Tom in a foul mood.

"I'm going to go find General Samson. Why don't you have a look around, and I'll give you a holler when I'm done," Mr. Keator said. The sawyer walked off toward the building where the tannery office was located.

The boy stood at the edge of the bustling operation, looking over the scene. The tannery consisted of a very long, open-sided main building next to the stream and an odd collection of smaller buildings around it. It was a bustling place with wagons coming and going and groups of men working at many tasks. Across the tannery yard, Matt could see some men unloading hides from a wagon, and nearer where he stood, a crew talked back and forth as they pitched hemlock bark off a wagon onto a growing pile. The men called the hemlock bark "tanbark."

One man's job was to drag the tanbark over to where a tired, sway-backed old horse walked in a circle at the end of a long wooden pole. The horse's slow circuits powered the rotations of a big stone wheel near the circle's center. Over and over again, the wheel passed over sheets of tanbark that the man dumped in its path. When the bark was shredded, another man raked it aside into heaps.

Watching the unfamiliar operations, Matt grew curious. Even though he had grown up only a few miles from the tannery, Matt really didn't know much about it—just some basic information and a few odd facts his father had told him. For instance, Matt knew the Samsonville tannery was a big one, but he remembered his father saying that further up in the Catskill Mountains, at a place called Edwardsville, there was a tannery with a building 500 feet long. Matt had been in a few barns more than 150 feet long, but he had a hard time imagining a building 500 feet long.

And with all the cows in these Catskill Mountain pastures, it had surprised Matt when his father told him that most of the cowhides for the Samsonville tannery came up in the holds of sailing ships from South America, a continent clear down in the southern hemisphere. Matt looked at the piles of hides and tried to imagine them as cows grazing under different stars on the other side of the world.

Matt strolled around the edge of the tannery until he saw a man working over a group of four vats set into the ground and sheltered by a tin roof. The vats steamed lazily, giving off a vapor that burned Matt's nose. The man held a long paddle and from time to time he walked around the vats poking at the hides soaking in the foamy broth. He looked to be in his middle years and was dressed like most other workmen, with the addition of a narrow brimmed leather hat and a thick leather apron that was stained and discolored.

"Phew! This is some smell," Matt commented, to catch the man's attention. The boy hoped he could strike up a conversation and ask the man some questions. When the man turned to Matt, he wore a perplexed look on his face.

"What smell would that be, lad?" the man asked with a grin.

At first Matt thought the man must be joking but then realized that his nose had probably been so overexposed to the tannery smells that he had stopped noticing them.

"What is it you're doing?" Matt asked.

"This here's the liming vat, lad," the man replied. "It's a soup of mineral lime and water we use to sweat the green hides—that means to dissolve the hair off the new hides. It's a caustic solution, so it'll burn. Don't get any on you."

Matt leaned cautiously over the vat and could see that the hair had all but dissolved on the hide that was visible in the foaming broth. He could only stand to look for a few moments before the caustic vapors drove him back with watering eyes.

"The fumes take some getting used to, I guess," the tannery man said. "My name's Bertram. And who might you be?"

As he spoke, the man doffed his leather hat and stuck out his hand. Matt noticed at once that Bertram was as bald as a hen's egg, and he wondered if the man's own green hide had been sweated by the stinging vapors rising from the vat.

"I'm Matt Quick," the boy said and shook the man's hand.

"Here, let me show you around the tannery," Bertram said. "These hides can stew for awhile without me.

"This here is mostly hemlock tanning, but we do some oak tanning too," Bertram began as they walked together toward the long main building. "The hemlock-tanned hides are redder in color than the oak-tanned ones and used for leather that doesn't need to be the toughest. Oh, hemlock-tanned leather is good for boot uppers and breeches, but you wouldn't want to walk on it or hitch a horse with it. Things like boot soles and harnesses are made from oak-tanned hides.

"Anyway, my job comes first. I get the hair off the hides, then we wash them good. The actual tanning process begins here at the tanning vats," Bertram said.

The two had entered the long open-sided building where men stood around rows of wooden vats set in the floor. Each vat was about six by eight feet in size, big enough to easily hold the hides and leave room for the tanning solution to circulate. The men stirred the vats with paddles to help the solution reach every part of the hides. Now and then a man would open a spigot to add steaming water or would shovel more of the shredded tanbark into the vats under the watchful eye of a supervising tanner.

"The tanbark contains an acid called tannic acid that cures the leather," Bertram explained. "I guess you can figure why it's called tanning.

"Each of these vats has a different strength tanning solution," Bertram continued as he pointed down the row of vats. "As the hides cure, we move them from one vat to another to get just the right tanning action. The whole process takes months. It's a true art, I tell you."

Next, Bertram took Matt down to the end of the line of vats where men were pulling the hides from the tanning vats and putting them in vats of clear water drawn directly from the creek. There the hides were rinsed again, and then the dirty, acidic rinse water was dumped back into the creek.

Matt could see that the whole operation depended on the stream. The water for the tannery was supplied by a network of channels built of stones and controlled by wooden gates. The channels took in the water upstream, and the men directed it as necessary to the woodfired boilers or to one or another of the vats. Then, when they wanted to replace the water, they opened other gates, and the water flowed out through other narrow stonework channels that dumped it back into the stream.

Matt was struck by the difference in the stream at the sawmill and here at the tannery. Upstream, the stream was clear and sparkling. Matt would not hesitate to stoop for a drink anywhere. And wherever the water gathered in a pool, small trout flashed below the surface.

But below the tannery, the water was cloudy and tea-colored. At the stream's edge, the tanning rinse had created puddles thick with a rank foam. The dumping of the rinse water wasn't the only cause. Scraps of tanbark covered the ground everywhere, and every time it rained, the runoff leached more tannic acid into the stream.

Matt knew the stream hadn't always been this way. When Matt's father was his own age, back before the tannery came in, this creek had been a great trout stream. His father had talked of catching thirty-one trout on one boyhood fishing trip. Now, everybody said the creek was all but dead for many miles downstream.

Matt thought of all the men working at the tannery. They were all his neighbors and many of them had wives and children to support. Without the tannery, where would they be? And he thought of all the leather things people used: shoes, leather breeches, harnesses, leather buckets, belts, leather gaskets ... the list was endless.

But it still made Matt sick to see the destruction of the stream. He didn't mention his feelings to Bertram, who was going on about the glories of tanning. The man was a bottomless well of facts and figures about tanning and the Samsonville Tannery.

"This here's one of the biggest tanneries in the country," Bertram said proudly. "In a good year, this tannery will use 8,000 cords of bark to tan something like 60,000 hides. General Samson's got 400 men working for him, counting the tanners, the bark peelers, and the teamsters who bring in the hides on wagons. We've got 75 horses and oxen hauling bark and hides and—" Suddenly the tanner stopped short.

"My hides! I almost forgot 'em! If I burn those hides in the lime, I'll be getting tanned myself," Bertram said. With a look of alarm the man hurried off, tossing Matt a wave over his shoulder.

As Matt watched Bertram dash off, he spotted Mr. Keator coming out of General Samson's office across the tannery yard. Matt turned his steps that way, hurrying past the drying shed where men were hanging the newly tanned and rinsed hides to drip dry in the shade. Mr. Keator saw Matt coming and waved.

"George, I'd like you to meet Matthew Quick—John Quick's only boy—who works for me at the mill now," Mr. Keator said as Matt walked up.

Matt recognized the general from a parade he had watched with his parents in Samsonville one fall day three years earlier. General Samson was one of the guests of honor on the reviewing stand as the militiamen marched by, and he had made a speech. The village people still talked proudly about that day and about the glowing article in the *Kingston Democratic Journal* afterward that had called Samsonville "a village humming with the sound of industry" and said "everything about the village gives evidence that thrift and happiness go hand in hand." General Samson was a big reason for it all.

The general was a compact, thickly built man with a hearty manner that fit his reputation as a businessman of boundless energy. He was dressed in a coat and a vest that seemed on the verge of exploding under the pressure of his barrel chest. General Samson shook Matt's hand warmly before he turned back to Mr. Keator.

"So we're square on this deal then, eh, George?" General Samson said. "I'm selling you the first choice of the logs my peelers have dropped over on Silas DuMont's lot near Sundown. I've got timber rights on some excellent first-growth timber there—oak and hemlock both. I think you'll be well pleased. After you've marked your allotment of timber, Silas's cousin, Avery DuMont, gets to mark the lesser quality logs."

"Yes, yes, I understand," Mr. Keator said. "Me and the boy here are going out there tomorrow to have a look and put our blaze on our logs. Come next January, I'll get my crew out there with the oxen, and we'll haul 'em out over the snow. By this time next year, I'll be selling you back the same logs as lumber."

General Samson laughed and slapped Mr. Keator on the back. He fished in his vest pocket for his big gold watch, took a long look at the time, and snapped the heavy lid shut. He harrumphed once or twice as if to announce he had something more to say.

"George, there's one more matter I must address," General Samson began in a more serious tone. "I think you know me to be a fair man who only judges others on the facts. I scorn gossip and hasty talk and the people who trade in it. It truly pains me to have to relate what I am about to say.

"You should take care in your dealings with Silas and Avery DuMont, George," General Samson said. "I have heard more than one troubling report from those who have done business with them recently."

"What kind of reports?" Mr. Keator asked.

"Oh, cords of firewood that were short or one-quarter dry-rotted. Sick cows sold as healthy ones. Barrels of rotten apples—things like that. Nothing serious enough to warrant the law getting involved," General Samson replied. "But it is worth a warning to a friend."

"Thanks for your words of concern, Henry," Mr. Keator said, "but I don't think I'll have any trouble with the DuMont boys."

"I trust not," General Samson said. "Well, I must be going. I have a meeting with the foreman in a few minutes."

The businessman shook Mr. Keator's hand, and Matt's as well, and strode away briskly.

"Matt, you'd best get home now and pack yourself a kit bag with a blanket and some necessaries. I'll meet you at the corner of Sundown Road at dawn. By tomorrow this time, we'll be camping." Mr. Keator's eyes had a faraway gleam as he worked the plug of tobacco in his jaw.

"Heck, maybe I can even get in some fishing! The Vernoy Kill is one pretty stream," the sawyer said. He smiled broadly and spit into the hemlock bark at his feet.

Matt's own feelings were mixed as he thought about the camping trip. He looked forward to the visit to the familiar woods, and Mr. Keator was right about the Vernoy Kill.

But he couldn't help remembering the last time he had camped there. That time he had been with his father.

"Well, I'll meet you at dawn then, Mr. Keator," Matt said.

Matt started up the tannery lane to Samsonville Road, but stopped and turned around as he heard his name called. "Goodbye, lad," the voice called from over at the liming vats.

Matt waved to Bertram, a distant figure in a leather hat and apron, then headed up the hill for the long walk home.

Chapter Seven

Among the Bark Peelers

M att dug through the trunk in the storeroom until he found his father's old canvas knapsack. He took the bag to the dooryard and turned it upside down to shake out the dirt and mouse droppings that he knew would have collected there since that last camping trip. To his surprise, out rolled a pure white pebble about the size and shape of a marble. The boy bent over and picked up the pebble between his thumb and forefinger. He held it up to his eye, and a sadness came over him as he remembered the day his father had found it.

Matt shook his head in an effort to banish the feeling. He tucked the pebble into his pocket and went back into the house. He laid the knapsack on the table and turned his attention to gathering the things he would need for the trip to the woods. First, Matt packed some dried beef, cheese, and apples to eat. To wear, he stuffed into the bag an extra shirt, a second pair of socks, and a warm sweater for nighttime. To sleep under, Matt rolled up a wool blanket and lashed it to the outside of the knapsack with a strip of buckskin. Finally, he tied a tin cup to the strap so he could dip himself a drink at any handy spring he passed on the hike.

Matt set out the knapsack on the table next to his bed, by the clothes he would wear. It was just dusk when he crawled into bed, and he lay awake thinking in the half-light. Matt got up from his bed and went to the little storeroom to get one more thing out of the trunk—a hunting knife with a staghorn handle and the name "John" burned into its leather sheath. He put the knife with the other gear and crawled back into bed. Now he could sleep.

The next day, in the gray first light, Matt set off down Samsonville Road with the knapsack swinging at his side and the hunting knife hanging from his belt. It was only a couple of miles to the Sundown Road corner, and he was there with time to spare. On the way, Matt had picked up an oak branch by the roadside. As he waited for Mr. Keator, he amused himself by whittling a row of notches and simple designs into the twisted wood shaft. By the time he saw Mr. Keator's wagon come around the bend, Matt had fashioned himself a fine walking stick. The boy put the hunting knife back in its sheath and waved to Mr. Keator.

As the wagon drew near, Matt saw Mr. Keator was at the reins of the wagon and Mrs. Keator sat next to him on the buckboard seat. She was a quiet, thin woman whose angular body suggested to Matt a split rail fence zigzagging across a field. Mrs. Keator's features were hidden in the dark under the broad brim of a sunbonnet, though the sun had yet to appear that day.

"We'll take the wagon until we get where the road gets steep," Mr. Keator explained, "then we'll set out on foot and my missus will bring the wagon back."

Matt slouched in the back of the wagon with his head resting on his knapsack as the wagon jounced along the rough road. In less than an hour, the road had left behind the farms and fields and had entered the woods and begun to climb. Finally, at a wide spot on the road, Mr. Keator gave a tug on the reins. The wagon slowed to a stop, and he handed the reins to his wife.

"Hop down, Matt. We're travelin' afoot from here," Mr. Keator said over his shoulder. The sawyer gave his wife an affectionate hug and climbed down from the buckboard seat. Matt climbed down too and waited as Mr. Keator came around to the back of the wagon and gathered up his own gear. The sawyer shouldered his pack and gave Matt a nod, and they set off. Behind them, they could hear the horse whinny and the noise of creaking wood and leather as Mrs. Keator turned the wagon around and headed it back to Samsonville.

The dawn had come and the sky was growing brighter, bringing the first hints of color into the still, gray woods. The birds were stirring and as Matt and Mr. Keator walked, they heard the first calls of finches and sparrows. Now the steep uphill road was little more than a pair of narrow wheel ruts through the trees.

"We'll follow the road almost to the sawmill at Vernoy Falls, then we'll cut over to the stream and follow it up until we get to the hemlock lot where the bark peelers are working," Mr. Keator said. "General Samson said he has more than a hundred boys working up there."

They had hiked about an hour-and-a-half uphill when the terrain flattened out. The road left the thick woods and was flanked on the right by a stone wall and a stump-riddled field—one of the new farms on the way to the little settlement at Vernoy Falls. They hiked on, and soon the distant rumbling sound of the waterfall began to reach Matt's ear. Mr. Keator stopped and pointed to a narrow wood road that branched off to the right. It was a rough and bumpy gash through the trees, where earth had been torn up by the recent passing of many men and horses. This way had not been here when Matt had last visited these woods with his father.

"Here's the turnoff to the hemlock woods," Mr. Keator said. "We're gettin' close now."

They followed the new path, and in another few minutes Matt and Mr. Keator began to hear the sound of the Vernoy Kill through the trees. This was the way Matt and his father had come to fish just a year before. Matt loved these woods. He knew that soon the open hardwood forest would give way to the hemlocks casting their dark shadows over the deep brooding pools where the big trout lived.

Matt recalled a particular pool in the stream up ahead. Last year, he and his father had come upon the spot on a sunny day after a rainy night. The hardwood places had dried up quickly that morning, but in the shade of the hemlocks, the night rain still hung in the air in a mist, and fat droplets clung to every hemlock needle. Matt and his father had happened upon the spot in the stream just as the late morning sun had found it, too. Before their eyes, a hundred shafts of sunlight had suddenly pierced through the intertwining hemlock branches, slicing the mist into glowing bands. The white sunlight had struck each crystal water droplet and shattered it into blue, red, and yellow pieces. The sunlight even had probed the depths of the pool, and Matt's father had glimpsed something shining in the water. He had reached into the water and plucked something from the bottom. It was the bright white pebble that Matt had found in the knapsack.

He recalled how he and his father had stood quietly and gazed at the rare and dazzling spectacle in the hemlock woods. But then the angle of the sun had changed, the light had vanished, and the hemlocks had regained sway in their green, dark domain. The boy remembered it all now as he reached into his pocket and rolled the white pebble reassuringly between his fingers.

As he and Mr. Keator walked farther along the wood road, Matt began to spot small hemlock patches among the hardwoods, then some larger hemlock trees. They were getting close to that magical spot in the stream, and Matt felt an inner joy as he remembered the time with his father. The boy craned his neck to see over the next rise. He wondered idly why the birds no longer sang here. Then, with a dawning sense of alarm, Matt detected an unfamiliar brightness through the trees.

Matt threw down the walking stick and broke into a run. His heart was pounding as he emerged through the edge of trees where the hemlock stand abruptly ended. Before him the wood road forded the stream at the pool where Matt and his father had stood in wonder just a year ago. The once pure stream was milky brown with the muddy runoff from the churned earth, and its flow was choked by broken branches and hemlock needles. Upstream and down, the brown water was crisscrossed by the trunks of countless downed hemlocks, each partly stripped of bark.

Matt felt a lump rising in his throat. So this was gone now too, he thought bitterly. Matt could not stop the sob that welled out of him, but he knew that Mr. Keator must not see him cry. The boy walked quickly ahead along the road that now was just a narrow aisle through the jumble

67

of downed trees. The peeled trees—still wet and slippery with sap—looked to Matt like pale flesh, like the exposed limbs of a once proud, now slaughtered, army. These were just trees, Matt reminded himself, but the image of dead soldiers stuck in his mind's eye.

He swallowed hard and drove this new grief out of his thoughts, then wiped his eyes on his sleeve and sat dejectedly on the stump of a huge old hemlock and waited for Mr. Keator to catch up.

A minute later, the sawyer, huffing and puffing, overtook Matt and sat down next to him on the stump. Mr. Keator's brow was sweating and he was out of breath. He mopped his forehead with a handkerchief and spit brown tobacco juice on the ground.

"Well, you're the young buck, aren't you, Mr. Quick?" Mr. Keator cracked. "How about shortening your step a bit so this old stag can keep up?"

The two rested for a few minutes and Matt noticed for the first time the familiar sounds of woodsmen working in the distance. He recognized the sharp sound of axes hitting live wood and an occasional muffled thud as a tree hit the ground.

"Looks like we're here anyway," Mr. Keator said. "Let's go see about our logs."

Matt and Mr. Keator walked on through the wasteland of downed trees bleaching in the sun. The road was lined with eight-foot-high piles of reddish hemlock bark, stacked in square piles with the outer side of the bark up. Here and there were mounds of oak bark, too, though there were far fewer of these. Matt knew the bark would wait there until winter, when it could be hauled out over the snow. The pair walked another five minutes or so before they saw men ahead working at the edge of the cut-over area. Beyond that line, the graceful hemlocks still waved majestically in the wind; on this side, they lay in jumbled heaps. If the hemlocks were soldiers, then this was the battle line, Matt thought.

Mr. Keator strode ahead and spoke to the first woodsman he saw. The man said something and pointed over to a cluster of bark-covered shanties in the near distance. Mr. Keator waved to Matt and walked off in the direction the man had pointed.

While he waited, Matt watched the bark peelers at work. The flow of sap that made it possible to peel the hemlock bark in sheets occurred only during the months of May and June, so the bark peelers worked fast. Matt had always noticed that the population of Samsonville increased on the Fourth of July, but it wasn't patriotism that brought the bark peelers into town. It was just the end of the peeling season.

Matt picked out one of the bark peelers to watch at work. He was a small bearded man in a very dirty brown shirt with leaves and twigs stuck to it from the hemlock sap. He had a kind of tall stocking cap that leaned over to the side, and he wore a hatchet hanging from his belt and carried other tools in his hands.

The man walked up to one of the hemlock trees and wasted no time getting to work. First the man girded the tree. Taking the short-handled hatchet from his belt, he chopped a gash all the way around the tree at its base. Even if the man walked away from the tree now, that gash alone was enough to bleed off the sap and kill the tree in a year, Matt knew. After cutting the gash, the man laid a measuring stick up against the tree and cut a second circular gash four feet higher up. Then he cut several up-and-down gashes between the two gashes that circled the trunk. The man wasted no motion, and the tasks went quickly.

Now the bark peeler set the hatchet aside and picked up a three-foot-long, flat-edged tool Matt recognized as a bark peeler's spud.Working in one of the vertical gashes, the bark peeler stuck the edge of the tool under the exposed edge of bark and worked the handle to pry the bark loose from the tree. He worked from the top to the bottom, and Matt saw the bark separate easily from the trunk, coming off in a curved sheet. The man worked his way around the tree, and soon had stripped all the bark off the lowest four-foot section of the trunk. The naked trunk looked slick and slippery.

Putting down the spud, the bark peeler picked up a long-handled felling ax. Now he could chop down the tree without spoiling any of the

Spud

marketable bark. The man swung the ax in steady arcs, not hurrying and not swinging with force. The ax was sharp, and it sunk deep into the wood with each blow. The bark peeler deeply notched one side of the tree, then moved around to finish the job from the other side. Soon, the top of the doomed tree swung unsteadily, and the man shouted a warning. There was a sharp cracking noise, and the tree toppled to the earth with a crash.

Immediately, the man was back at the tree with his hatchet cutting more gashes around the trunk. The man worked his way up to the first set of big branches, which were about a third of the way up the tree, and went back to peeling the bark with the spud. Above where the branches started, you couldn't get a good-sized piece of bark, and the bark peelers usually didn't peel the top two-thirds of the tree. Matt watched the man peel off the sheets of bark, exposing more and more of the slick white trunk. The bark peeler stacked the bark with the rough side up so it wouldn't curl. The sight of the man stripping the tree reminded Matt of illustrations he had seen in books of New England whalers peeling the blubber off the carcasses of whales.

Mr. Keator had been gone awhile now, and Matt looked around for him among the workmen. Soon, he spotted the sawyer over by the bark shanties, and he walked over to see what was going on.

"The DuMont boys are off in another part of the wood lot, but they should be back soon," Mr. Keator said.

"I've already seen some mighty fine timber, though, including some nice oak that's big enough to quarter-saw. We'll get a good price for it as lumber," he added enthusiastically.

71

"Why is one big tree any better than a lot of littler ones?" Matt asked. "And what do you mean by quarter-sawing?"

Mr. Keator stooped, picked up a twig, and sketched a circle in the dirt representing a cross section of a log. Then he filled it in with more circles representing the growth rings of the tree.

"To get the most planks out of a log, we usually just cut them one after another in parallel slices without regard to the grain of the wood," Mr. Keator said, and he drew parallel lines cutting through the cross section. He pointed out how each plank had differing lengths of growth rings in its cross section. Only the board that went through the center of the log had short, equal segments of the rings, and the most even grain.

"You get the widest boards this way, but the boards shrink across the grain when they dry, and because the sections of grain are all different lengths, the board can warp out of shape," he explained. "It's especially true for

Plain Cut vs. Quarter Sawing

the hardwoods, like oak. Leave a green oak plank in the sun and it'll bend up like the rocker off a rocking chair."

Then Mr. Keator sketched another cross section, this time cut into four equal quarters—like four pieces of pie. In each quarter he drew parallel lines running toward the center of the cross section.

"In quarter-sawing, you start by cutting the log into four quarters. Then you cut your planks toward the center of the tree—perpendicular to the growth rings. You get more waste and you don't get the widest boards, but the boards you do get don't warp because the sections of grain are short and equal. With logs as big as these are, we can quarter-saw and still get wide boards—and I can charge a higher price for the better quality."

The sawyer's lesson was interrupted by the approach of two men. They were the DuMont cousins, Silas and Avery. Silas, the landowner, led the way. He was a thin man dressed in a soiled vest and badly worn felt hat, and he had a long splinter of wood stuck out of the corner of his mouth like a toothpick. Silas's cousin Avery walked behind. He had evidently been working at the job of bark peeling, and his shabby clothes were stiff with dried sap. Avery walked with the bone-weary rocking gait Matt had seen in many of the long-time bark peelers, and his eyes flitted this way and that like a nervous bird. Matt disliked both men immediately.

Silas greeted Mr. Keator, then led them off toward a shanty. Matt could see the rude structure was made of poles lashed together and shingled with pieces of hemlock bark too small to sell to the tannery. In the dark interior, he could barely make out bunks made of poles and rope.

There were a dozen or more of the shanties spread through the trees, each with its own ring of blackened stones for a campfire. These were the bark peelers' temporary homes.

Silas entered one of the shanties and came out with a map and some other scraps of paper.

"We're standing here, George," said Silas, jabbing his finger at the map. "Most of the prime first-growth timber you'll be wanting is over this way. You and your boy can mark yours today, and then tomorrow Avery can go in and mark his."

Avery's eyes flitted briefly toward Mr. Keator and Matt, and a smile flickered across his lips.

"Now, just so's we know whose logs is whose, you blaze your logs like this," Silas resumed, and he drew a rough **X** on a piece of paper with a pencil. "Now Avery here will mark his logs this way." Silas sketched a **Z**, then connected the diagonal ends to make a rough hourglass shape on the paper.

Mr. Keator was looking intently at the map, but Matt was standing behind him eyeing the DuMont cousins. The boy saw the DuMonts exchange a sidelong glance, and he thought he detected Silas smile crookedly and wink at his cousin Avery, who was shuffling his feet and acting nervous. Matt thought back to what General Samson had said at the tannery, and he looked at the blaze marks again more closely. Suddenly, it dawned on him.

"Mr. Keator, there's something over here I want to show you," Matt said, tugging on the sawyer's sleeve.

"Not now, Matt, I'm busy," Mr. Keator replied.

"This is important, Mr. Keator," Matt insisted. The

sawyer raised his eyebrows and looked sharply at Matt, but something in Matt's eyes told him to go along.

"Excuse me, boys, while I humor the young 'un," Mr. Keator said.

Matt led Mr. Keator about ten steps away, and the two squatted with their backs to the DuMont cousins. Matt unsheathed his father's hunting knife and quickly sketched some shapes in the dirt. They spoke in low voices for a minute, and Mr. Keator nodded and stood up. The sawyer rubbed out the sketches in the dirt with the toe of his boot and turned back to face the DuMont cousins. Mr. Keator frowned and worked his chaw for minute. Then he spit decisively in the dirt and strode back to finish up his business with the two men from Sundown.

A half-hour later, Mr. Keator was in high good humor as he and Matt measured and marked the logs for the mill. The sawyer chuckled to himself when he thought back on the encounter with the DuMonts. He grinned over at Matt every time he blazed a log.

"Another piece of prime timber blazed with 'Matt's mark'!" the sawyer said as his hatchet flashed in the late afternoon sunlight.

Matt's stomach had already been growling for an hour when Mr. Keator finally signaled a stop to set up camp. As Matt tended their small campfire at the edge of the woods, Mr. Keator rigged a fishing pole using a springy sapling he had cut and a hook and line he had brought along. For bait, he found some grubs under a rotten log. The man was as excited as any schoolboy.

"Wish me luck, Matt," called out Mr. Keator as he started

off upstream with a jaunty step. But it wasn't long before Mr. Keator came back grumbling and shaking his head.

"There's aren't no fish in that stream no more. The water's all riled, and it's too hot for the fish now that the stream's out in broad daylight," he complained.

Mr. Keator looked out over the campfire at the expanse of cut-over woodlands. He muttered and spit into the fire in disgust.

"Blast it! This used to be a pretty spot, but I'll be dead and gone before it will be again. It's a shame to cut it over like this," Mr. Keator said, heaving a sigh. "But I guess a man's got to make his living."

Later, Matt lay on the blanket on his bed of hemlock boughs and gazed into the embers of the dying fire. He rolled the white pebble in his palm and thought about the spoiled place in the stream where he had stood with his father and about Mr. Keator's ruined fishing trip. Then he considered what Mr. Keator had said about making a living. Matt wondered if making a living must always mean sacrificing the place you live and the things you live for.

Chapter Eight

Matt's Mark

L
ike a stage actor in his big scene, Mr. Keator was relishing this moment in the limelight. The sawyer stood in the millyard with his hands on his hips and his feet widespread and chewed his plug as his eyes swept over his small audience. He was getting to the good part of the story of his run-in with the DuMonts and wanted to tell it to best effect, and that required a bit of dramatic tension.

Around the sawyer, his audience was seated on stacks of lumber and barrels. There was Basil, Ned, and Tom, of course, and General Samson and some of his crew had come up from the tannery to hear Mr. Keator's tale too. A few men from the village even had been drawn to the sawmill by the rumor that Mr. Keator had a yarn to tell. Mr. Keator knew that once the story was out to these men, it wouldn't take long for the rest of Samsonville to hear about the way George Keator and Matt Quick had made fools of those shifty DuMont boys.

At last Mr. Keator judged that the suspense had built enough. He squinted at the audience, spit in the sawdust for effect, and picked up his story.

"So there we are, and Silas is saying, 'Here's your mark, George,' and he draws an X on the paper. Then he says, 'and here's Avery's mark,' and he draws a Z and connects the ends to make a kind of hourglass shape," Mr. Keator recounted. "He drew it real casual, like there wasn't nothing to it, but Matt seen right off what was up."

The sawyer didn't mind the blank faces around him. They didn't get it yet, but he'd aroused their curiosity and they were all ears.

"So Matt, he gives me a nudge, and we go over to a spot a way's off, and he draws the two blazes in the dirt with a knife—first the X and then the hourglass," Mr. Keator continued.

"'Mr. Keator,' Matt whispers to me, 'I think those DuMonts are trying to cheat you. See, all you have to do is add two ax strokes to your X and it looks like their mark. We can mark all the best logs, and Avery can come along behind us and change all the marks to his.'"

"So then, Matt scratched a line between the two top tips of the X and the two bottom tips and, sure enough, it's the hourglass," Mr. Keator explained. "It was easy to reason that after Avery re-marked our logs, he could have just gone around putting our mark on a lot of the other poorer logs." Mr. Keator stopped talking and scanned the faces of his audience again as the point of the story sunk in.

"But how can you be sure the DuMonts really were going to do that?" Tom asked.

Mr. Keator grinned to himself as he thought back on the incident.

"A good question, Tom. I asked that one myself. So Matt said, 'How about we just offer to swap marks with the DuMonts and see what happens?' 'Right,' I said. One mark is as good as another. If they accept the swap, no harm done. If they won't swap—well, that tells you something," Mr. Keator said. The sawyer paused again for effect, as the men all looked at each other and nodded.

"So what did they do, George?" General Samson finally asked impatiently.

"Well, here's where it gets good, Henry," Mr. Keator said. "I walked right up to those DuMonts and I said, 'Well, boys, I feel a little bad about these marks. Here, I'm getting the better logs and the better blaze, too. I can make my X in a couple of strokes, but it'll take Avery twice as many to make his mark. I feel like I'm taking an unfair advantage. What do you say we swap marks, Avery?'

"Well, old Avery's eyes got real big, and he looked over at his sharpie cousin for a clue, but Silas's face is a blank. He's just chewing his toothpick and looking straight ahead. So Avery hems and haws and finally says, 'No, no, that's all right, I'll keep my mark.' Well, I insisted a little, just to make him squirm some more, and then insisted a little more just to be sure. But no, Avery won't switch, and then I knew Matt was right."

Mr. Keator's eyes twinkled as he directed a mischievous smile at his audience.

"So then I decided to have myself a little fun with the DuMont boys," the sawyer continued. "I composed a speech on the spot. I said, 'You know, boys, I just can't take advantage of poor Avery this way. Here, I'll be tripping through the logs making my easy mark, and he'll be trailing along behind taking twice as long with each mark and doing twice the work. It's just not fair to him. Any man that would take unfair advantage of another man in a business deal like that is lower than a highway robber. At least a robber comes at you straight ahead with his gun drawn and announces his intentions. A business cheat comes at you from your blind side of trust.'

"Well, the DuMonts are looking at each other funny

now. All this talk about the marks is making them edgy, but they're trying to keep from giving themselves away," Mr. Keator continued.

"I said, 'Avery, if you won't swap marks, then I guess I'll just add a couple more ax strokes to my blaze so we can at least start out even.' I grabbed Silas's paper and drew some marks connecting the top and bottom of my X. Then I made a face like I was surprised and I looked straight at the DuMonts. 'Well, this mark won't do,' I said. 'It looks just the same as yours, Avery! Next winter my crew might take some of your logs by mistake. We can't have that!'

"So that set me off again and I sermonized them up and down about honesty in business. I quoted the law, brought in the Scriptures, and told them what my pappy taught me on his knee. I put old Reverend McHarlow in the shade, if you must know," Mr. Keator said.

"By now Silas is looking as pale as a trout belly, and Avery's eyes are jumping around like a one-legged grasshopper. I just kept sermonizing, and looking from one to the other, and giving each of them a look hard enough to dry up a cow," Mr. Keator said.

"They were squirming, I tell you. And the best part of it was that the two scalawags couldn't even protest. They had to play dumb to save face. They knew if they made a peep, then they've as much as confessed their scheme. They both just stood there sweating like a couple of pigs in August."

The sawyer chuckled to himself. The men in the mill-yard all grinned at each other as they pictured Mr. Keator giving Silas and Avery DuMont the tongue-lashing of their lives and the two confused Sundown men standing there as meek and mute as schoolboys caught in a prank they couldn't admit.

"I tell you, those DuMont boys were fish in a barrel," Mr. Keator said giddily. "They knew that I knew, and I knew that they knew that I knew, and there wasn't anything they could do about it."

Mr. Keator was laughing full out now, and the men started to laugh too, slowly at first, but then harder as they pictured how ridiculous the DuMonts must have looked. The laughter fed on itself and soon grew into a general hilarity, and the men rocked on their bottoms and slapped their thighs. No one laughed harder than Mr. Keator. The sawyer laughed until he held his sides, and then he caught his breath and continued his tale.

"So finally I crossed out their marks on the paper and drew an <u>M</u> and underlined it for emphasis. 'This here is Matt's mark,' I told them, 'and it's the mark of the Keator sawmill from now on.' They said fine, whatever I wanted, and suddenly they realized that they had business elsewhere, and off they went to lick their wounds," Mr. Keator said.

The sawyer wiped a tear of mirth from his eye and shook his head. "I tell you, boys, it was a day the DuMonts will not soon forget, and I won't either."

General Samson wiped his own eyes with a handkerchief he had pulled from his breast pocket and stuck out his hand to Mr. Keator. "George, let me shake your hand," he said. "Laying into those boys like you did may have been the best thing anybody ever did for them. Maybe now they'll mend their ways. You were just lucky Matt spotted the trick. He's one bright boy."

"It was sharp of the boy to see it," the sawyer agreed. "If he hadn't, the trick wouldn't have been caught. Next winter, the crew in the woods would have just collected up whatever logs had the right mark. I wouldn't be there to spot something amiss. Next spring I would have been standing here wondering why my logs looked so much better in the woods than in the millyard."

Suddenly, a question occurred to General Samson, and he looked around the millyard as if searching for the answer.

"By the way, George, where is Matt today?" General Samson asked.

"Oh, I gave him the day off, Henry. He earned it," Mr. Keator said.

Standing near the lumber pile, Tom overheard, and his eyes widened in amazement. During the sawing season, Sundays and Independence Day and funerals were the only days off he had ever known. And Mr. Keator used to say that the only way you could get the whole of a funeral day off was if it was your own funeral.

Chapter Nine

Matt Takes a Plunge

r. Keator stood in the dry flume brandishing the slender birch whip as if it were a schoolmaster's pointer. He pointed in the direction of the mill-wheel, hooked a thumb in his suspenders, cleared his throat, and began to speak. Suddenly, Matt felt like he was back in school, not at the sawmill.

"So, as I was saying, Matt, this here is an overshot wheel," Mr. Keator said. "It's the most efficient kind of waterwheel because it uses the actual weight of the water to turn the wheel."

Mr. Keator got down on one knee and pointed at the water-tight compartments—buckets, he called them—that lined the rim of the wheel.

"The water comes in at the top—that's why it's called an overshot wheel. Then, as the water fills the bucket at the top of the wheel, the weight starts the wheel turning. Then the next bucket fills up, and then the next behind that. As each bucket reaches the bottom, it dumps its load of water," Mr. Keator went on. "See, on your bigger streams, you can use an undershot wheel, which just turns by the force of the stream flowing under it, but this small creek doesn't have that much flow, so ..."

Matt smiled and pretended interest as Mr. Keator droned on. The boy already knew what an overshot millwheel was, and it was obvious to anyone how it worked. Mr. Keator leaned out over the falls, spit tobacco juice into the white water, and resumed his lecture. Now Matt could see the sawyer's lips moving, but he could not make out the words over the roar of the falls. The boy simply nodded his head whenever the sawyer looked his way.

Mr. Keator had been giving Matt these lectures ever since the trip to the hemlock woods. Apparently, the incident with the DuMont boys had made Matt Mr. Keator's favorite. The fact that Matt had saved the sawyer from being cheated probably had a lot to do with it, but Matt thought it more likely that Mr. Keator was grateful for the story of the run-in with the DuMonts. It was a yarn he could embellish and repeat for years to come.

Whatever his motive, Mr. Keator showed his favor by taking a sudden and deep interest in Matt's education as a sawyer. First, he had taken Matt through the sawmill and explained to him the workings of the machinery that transferred the power of the turning millwheel to the saw and to the log carriage. Then he showed Matt just where all the parts to be greased were. After that, the sawyer put Matt in charge of the greasing. Matt appreciated the new responsibility, not because he liked the job but because making the rounds with the grease can took him away from the scrap pile at least some of the time.

There had been other lessons too. One day, after noticing that the newly cut planks were beginning to look a little wavy, Mr. Keator squinted along the spinning disk of the saw and swore in mild disgust. He signaled to Ned to shut the gate to the flume. Then, with a big wrench and a helping hand from Basil, the sawyer removed the big saw and laid it out flat on the sawmill floor. Mr. Keator beckoned Matt over to show him another piece of sawyer's lore: how to tune up a saw with a wooden mallet.

"A circular saw isn't perfectly flat, boy. It's actually slightly dished," Mr. Keator explained. "You see, there's a force that is created by an object spinning. If you swing a bucket in a circle over your head, you can feel it. That force will even keep the water in that bucket when it's upside down. The books call it centrifugal force.

"If your saw was completely flat, that centrifugal force would cause the spinning saw to vibrate, and it wouldn't cut in a straight line," he continued. "The way the sawyer defeats centrifugal force is by using a saw that is slightly dished. Then, when the saw is spinning, the force uses itself up making the dished saw flatten out.

"When the dish shape goes out of the saw—like it has with ours—the sawyer has to hammer it back in with a mallet," Mr. Keator concluded. "It's called tuning the saw."

With that, the sawyer started to beat on the saw. As Matt watched, the sawyer pounded for a few minutes, then squinted at the saw from different angles, then beat on it some more. Mr. Keator kept right on talking through the whole process but Matt couldn't make out a word over the noisy clanging.

After a half hour of banging, Mr. Keator sighted along the saw from every angle and nodded his satisfaction. Matt's ears rang, and he could not see any difference between the saw before the tuning and after. But when they had remounted the saw and gone back to sawing, the saw cuts were arrow-straight again.

Matt appreciated the new variety of sawmill tasks that went along with being Mr. Keator's favorite, but there was a bad side to it, too. It angered Tom to see so much fuss made over Matt, and the bigger boy took to belittling Matt more than ever. When the two boys were working together—which was most of the time—Tom made his anger known by small acts of spite. If the boys shared a burden, such as a stout log or a pile of flitches, Tom would drop his end without warning. More than once, Matt went home with bruises on his shoulder from that trick. Or if they were shoveling sawdust, Tom was always sure to get a handful of it down the neck of Matt's shirt, where it stuck to the boy's sweaty back and itched terribly. Matt was convinced Tom did these things on purpose, but he never said anything to the bigger boy.

One hot June day, Mr. Keator ordered the saw stopped, as usual, so he could sharpen it with the file. The saw filing was a daily midmorning ritual, and one performed only by Mr. Keator. Matt picked up the grease can and began making his rounds as the rest of the sawmill crew headed down to Mr. Keator's well pump for a cold drink. Mr. Keator looked up from his filing and beckoned Matt over.

"Matt, I think it's about time I showed you how to sharpen a saw," the sawyer said. "It takes a good eye and sure touch and, if you're going to be a sawyer someday, it's an art you have to master."

Matt put down the grease can and watched the sawyer run the file carefully over the saw teeth. Matt wondered where Mr. Keator had gotten the idea he wanted to be a sawyer—it was the farthest thing from his own mind. But, as always, Matt appreciated Mr. Keator's good intentions, so he watched attentively and asked the questions that occurred to him. Then Mr. Keator handed the file to Matt, showed him how to hold it against the teeth, and guided his hands through several practice strokes. In a few minutes, they had sharpened all but a few of the teeth. Mr. Keator never let the saw get too dull, so it never took long to restore the edge.

"Matt, I'm going to run down to the house for a minute. How about you take the file and finish off the last couple of teeth for me?" Mr. Keator said.

Matt was dumbfounded. He had never seen anybody but Mr. Keator take a file to the saw before, not even Basil.

"Are you sure, Mr. Keator?" Matt said. "I might make a mistake and spoil a saw tooth."

"Nonsense," Mr. Keator said, waving away Matt's reluctance. "You're a quick learner. Just do it like we practiced."

Matt took the big iron file, placed it against one of the teeth, and looked over his shoulder at Mr. Keator to see if he was holding it right.

"That looks good, Matt. You go ahead, and I'll be right back," Mr. Keator said.

Matt filed slowly at first, but as the tooth began to gleam under his strokes, he gained confidence and picked up his pace. At last, he blew the tiny metal filings away and squinted at the tooth just as he had seen Mr. Keator do. The tooth looked just as sharp as the ones the sawyer had done. Matt began filing another tooth, now with more assurance. Suddenly, he heard an angry voice directed at him.

"What do you think you're doing, schoolboy?" the voice demanded, and Matt looked up to see Tom glaring at him.

"Nobody touches the saw but Mr. Keator. You know that," Tom said.

"But Mr. Keator said—" Matt started to reply, but the bigger boy snatched the file out of his hand.

"Never mind. You give me that," Tom said, and he waved the file under Matt's nose. "You were the teacher's pet in school, and now you think you're the teacher's pet here, but when Mr. Keator sees that you've messed with the saw, he'll knock you down a peg or two."

When Tom saw the sawyer walking up the lane with Basil and Ned, he smiled smugly, but the smile faded fast when Mr. Keator spoke.

"Matt, did you finish sharpening the saw like I told you?" the sawyer asked. There was an uncomfortable silence as Matt tried to think of a way to answer without putting Tom in a bad light. Tom spoke up first.

"I can finish up for you, Mr. Keator. I've been watching you file that saw for the past three seasons. I know how to do it," Tom said.

Mr. Keator looked at Tom in surprise.

"Well, that's so, Tom, you have looked on for a while. The fact is, I'm not sure you have a careful enough touch," Mr. Keator said. "But, say, if you're interested in learning, you can start by practicing on that old saw we wore out and stuck in the shed."

Tom nodded and grinned bitterly. His eyes swept over the others, and he spoke through clenched teeth.

"Oh, I get it. I'm fine for mule work, but not good enough for any better job. Well, if you think this schoolboy is better than me, then ... then ..." Tom fumbled for words.

"Then, the lot of you are all wet!" he finally blurted. Tom threw the file down in the sawdust, turned his back, and stalked away.

Mr. Keator didn't know what to make of the outburst. He just looked at the others and shrugged his shoulders. But Matt thought that Tom had a reason to be mad. He should get the first crack at the better jobs—he'd worked there longer and he had earned it. Now this new incident would just make Tom even harder to get along with. Matt's grandmother had said that if Matt were kind enough, long enough, Tom would come around. Matt hoped she was right, but he couldn't help wondering how long was long enough.

Shimmering waves of heat rose off the sawmill's tin roof. The high afternoon sun beat down on the sawmill crew as they loaded the last of the heavy sap-coated planks into the bed of the wagon. Their shirts were soaked with sweat and stuck to their backs. As they waited for Mr. Keator's next instructions, they wearily waved away the flies that buzzed around their heads.

"Blazes, it's hot!" Mr. Keator said as he mopped at his own forehead with the rag from his back pocket. "I think we're done. You boys, take a blow in the shade while I go find the lumber order to make sure."

Mr. Keator walked off as the workers sat in the shade, out of the sun and away from the buzzing flies. No one spoke as the men hung their heads over their knees and closed their eyes. They were too hot and tired to speak, much less move.

Matt had never been so hot and thirsty, and he knew the others were, too. A drink of water sure would taste good now. Matt had an idea. The boy got up and walked down the lane to Mr. Keator's well house. He worked the pump handle until the clear cold water began to gush from the spout. In a minute, he had filled an oaken bucket to the brim with ice-cold water. Matt grabbed the tin cup that hung in the wellhouse, picked up the bucket by its rope handle, and started back to where the others still sat, heads down, making the most of their rest in the shade.

Maybe this could be one of those acts of kindness that his grandmother said would win Tom over, Matt thought, and he turned his weary steps toward Tom to offer the boy the first drink from the bucket. Matt was bone-tired and the bucket was heavy and his steps dragged as he walked across the millyard. He was within a step or two of Tom when his foot came across a tree root concealed by the sawdust underfoot. Suddenly, Matt sprawled forward, and instead of a drink, Tom got the whole bucket of ice-cold water dumped over him.

"Aaagh!" Tom cried out, and he sprang to his feet.

Basil looked over at Tom, sputtering and drenched, and let go with a burst of laughter. "Say, Tom, just who was it you said was all wet?" Basil cracked.

Basil always appreciated his own jokes more than anyone else did. He slapped his knee and surrendered to uncontrollable laughter. Ned became infected with laughter too, and the two men rocked back and forth holding their sides.

Red-faced with rage, Tom fixed his eye on Matt, lying on the ground where he had fallen. Seizing the front of Matt's shirt, Tom dragged the boy to his feet and thrust his snarling face inches from Matt's own. Matt felt a strange coldness fill his insides as he looked up into Tom's blazing eyes.

"You did that on purpose, schoolboy!" Tom yelled

angrily, and water sprayed Matt's face. "Now we'll see how you like it!"

With that, Tom spun Matt around and grabbed the seat of his pants. Swinging the boy once like a bucket of slops to the hogs, Tom heaved Matt out over the millpond. Matt came down headfirst in about two feet of water at the edge of the pond. Basil's laughter reached new heights as Matt floundered in the shallow water and mud. The boy's head was coated with thick mud and he could feel it ooze down his face. Matt was grateful for the mud. It hid the tears welling up in his eyes.

"What the devil's gotten into you, Tom!" Mr. Keator shouted as he hurried over. The sawyer had heard the laughter and had seen what Tom did. Mr. Keator looked at Matt sitting in the muddy water and then turned and stared straight at Tom.

"Blast it, Tom! Ever since Matt came here you've had a chip on your shoulder big enough to saw a bridge timber!" Mr. Keator said. "Well, you've just lost yourself a half-day's pay! You get out of here now, and when you come back tomorrow, I don't want no more trouble out of you, you hear? Now git!"

Mr. Keator punctuated his angry outburst with a profanity and bolt of tobacco juice at Tom's feet.

Tom said nothing. He glared at Matt and stomped off. Basil laughed behind his hand as Matt rinsed the mud from his face, got to his feet in the millpond, and waded back to dry land.

"Matt, you go home too and get out of those muddy clothes," Mr. Keator said in a gentler tone.

Without a word to anyone, Matt turned his steps down the lane to Samsonville Road. He could feel his shoes squish with every step, and he prayed that the leather wouldn't be ruined by the drenching. They were his only shoes except for the church pair.

As Matt walked glumly home, he felt his clothes heavy and soggy against his skin. He stopped by the roadside and took off his shoes and stuffed them with dry grass to help soak up the water. Matt lay in the grass to let the sun dry his clothes and brooded about what had happened. After a while, his clothes were just a little damp—except for his shoes—and he resumed the walk home. He walked barefoot, carrying his wet shoes in his hand.

At last, Matt cleared the hill and saw the little cottage across the field. His grandmother, in a wide-brimmed straw hat, was staking the tomato plants in the garden plot. Matt's clothes were dry now, and he stooped and put his damp shoes back on his feet. Matt didn't intend to tell his grandmother what had happened at the sawmill. There was nothing she could do about it anyway, and she would just worry, the boy reasoned.

Later that night, Matt lay awake in bed for a long time. He had rubbed neatsfoot oil into the leather of his shoes, so they were saved. His other problem would be harder to fix. The boy could not get the day's events out of his mind. He was ashamed that the men at the sawmill had seen him handled like that. Worst of all, Matt had to admit to himself that he had grown to fear Tom. How could he go back to the sawmill tomorrow and face them all after this humiliation? What would he do if Tom came at him again?

As Matt lay in bed wide-eyed, all his doubts and uncertainties resolved into one unanswerable question. "I wonder what my father would tell me to do?" the boy thought.

Chapter Ten

Old Bob

Matt hesitated at the entrance to the sawmill lane. He shuffled his feet in the dust and again rehearsed in his mind the tough speech he planned to make the next time he had any trouble with Tom. Matt started up the lane with the words drilling in his mind like troops he'd mustered against a foe. When he came within sight of the sawmill, Matt saw Tom, Ned, and Basil talking over by the skids. Matt thought he saw Tom glance his way briefly and then say something to Basil. Basil laughed, and the feeble words in Matt's mind scattered like a routed army.

"They're talking about me," Matt thought, and the boy felt the strange coldness inside again—a coldness he recognized as belonging to the fear and shame he felt. The boy didn't know how he could face Tom after the dunking in front of everybody. He dreaded even more the amused and mocking looks he was sure would be exchanged behind his back.

Matt stood in the lane trying to rally his courage to walk the rest of the way up the hill to the mill. His glum thoughts were interrupted by the sound of someone calling his name. It was Mr. Keator.

"Matt—come over here," the sawyer repeated. "I want to talk to you a minute."

Mr. Keator was at the edge of the millyard next to the wagon they had loaded with planks the day before. The horses were hitched to the wagon, and the sawyer was holding the reins in his hands. As Matt walked up, he thought that Mr. Keator looked uncomfortable.

"Matt, I'd like you to take the wagon we loaded yesterday over to the Hornbeck place," the sawyer began. "You know where it is, don't you? Up off Brown's Road?"

Matt nodded. He knew Mr. Hornbeck from church. The farmer owned one of the more prosperous farms around Samsonville. Matt reached for the reins, but the sawyer made no move to hand them over. There was an awkward silence as the boy waited for Mr. Keator to finish what he had to say.

"There's another thing," the sawyer continued. "Hornbeck's got a crew up there getting ready for a barn raising. He's short-handed, so I told him I'd send you up there for a spell to help out. We're pretty well caught up on our orders here, and I can spare you for a while."

So this was why Mr. Keator looked uncomfortable. He was sending Matt away. The boy studied the sawyer's face for a clue to his thoughts, but all he saw was the plug of chewing tobacco bobbing up and down in Mr. Keator's cheek.

"I—I thought you could use a little change from the sawmill," Mr. Keator added after a pause. "But don't worry, I'll get word to you when we need you back here."

"All right, Mr. Keator," Matt said. The boy felt mixed emotions. He was glad to be getting away from the sawmill and from Tom, but he was sure he was being sent away because Mr. Keator thought him too weak to hold his own with the others. It made Matt feel more ashamed.

"When you get to Hornbeck's, ask for Old Bob. He's the boss of the barn building crew," Mr. Keator said. "Tell him I sent you."

The sawyer smiled. He gave Matt a reassuring clap on the shoulder and chewed his plug thoughtfully. It seemed to Matt that Mr. Keator wanted to say something more but couldn't think of what it was.

"So I guess that's it," the sawyer said finally. "You be on your way now, and we'll be seeing you back here soon enough."

Matt took the reins and climbed up onto the wagon seat. He flicked the reins and the wagon lurched to a start. Matt waved to Mr. Keator but fought the urge to look back to see if Tom and the others were watching him leave. As the wagon rattled along Matt brooded about this new turn of events.

The trip to the Hornbeck farm took more than an hour, and it was getting near midmorning when Matt at last turned the wagon down the long lane, bordered by maple trees, that led to a big white clapboard farm house with green shutters and a wide porch. As the wagon rolled by the house, he saw Mrs. Hornbeck, topped by her familiar starched white bonnet, hanging sheets on the clothesline. Mrs. Hornbeck was reputed to be a fussy woman who liked things neat. Even her privy had lace curtains, the rumor was in town. Matt smiled as he spotted the small outhouse with the half-moon shape cut into the door. Sure enough, dainty white curtains fluttered in the tiny window.

The lane continued past the house and into the farm-yard, where a flock of chickens scattered noisily at the approach of the wagon. The wagon rolled slowly past the chicken coop and then past Hornbeck's cow barn, its doors standing open to reveal rows of empty stalls.

Now Matt could hear the singsong sound of handsaws and the irregular rhythm of hammers and axes. Ahead he saw a row of trees and an opening in the stone fence. The lane curved left through the opening, passed an open wagon shed, and ended at a wide expanse of rolling fields, divided by stone fences. There, at the edge of the first field, was the site of the new barn.

Matt could see stacks of lumber and piles of bluestone and a half-dozen men working at various tasks. One shirt-less man was laying up the barn's stone foundation, while another split shingles from a short, stout log. There were other men hewing timbers and sawing lumber. Then Matt spotted a stout, red-faced man in a straw hat smoking a pipe with a curved stem. It was Farmer Hornbeck. The boy reined in the horses, set the wagon brake, and jumped down.

"Hello, Mr. Hornbeck," Matt called out.

"Well, hello, Matthew. Good to see you," the farmer replied as he waved Matt over.

"Mr. Keator at the sawmill sent me over with this lum-ber and to help with the barn raising. He said I should ask for Old Bob when I got here," Matt said.

"Yes, yes, of course. It's a pleasure to have you here," Mr. Hornbeck said. "You can just leave the wagon there, Matt. One of my boys will take care of it. You'll find Old Bob over there."

Mr. Hornbeck pointed toward a big chestnut tree at the edge of the field where a small, gray-haired man wielded a broad ax over a timber. The old man swung the ax in short regular arcs, sending out a steady stream of wood chips. Around him were hewed timbers in various states of completion, and the ground was covered with wood chips. Matt walked over to the man and stood for a moment watching before he found his voice and spoke.

"Excuse me, sir? My name's Matthew Quick. Mr. Keator sent me over to help get ready for the barn raising. He told me to see you when I got here," Matt said.

The old carpenter paused over the half-hewn log and looked up at Matt through a shock of gray hair. The first thing Matt saw was a pair of eyes as black as coal, set in a lean, lined face. Old Bob's eyes glinted like coal, too, as though flecked with the same mica chips. But when the old man smiled, wrinkles radiated from the corners of those eyes to add a humorous quality that softened any hard effect. He wore a neat gray moustache like a brush on his upper lip.

Old Bob was lightly built—not much bigger than Matt, really—but Matt could see ropey sinews in the man's fore-arms, and there was strength evident in the way he handled the broad ax. The carpenter was dressed in a faded and worn blue work shirt and trousers that showed the effects of many washings. The trousers were oddly belled at the cuffs and were patched at the knees, but the patches were neatly stitched, and Old Bob's suspenders seemed almost new. The overall impression was of a man whose nature was marked by neatness and practicality.

"Well, Matthew, I'm pleased to meet you. And you can just call me Bob like everybody else does," the man said as he offered his hand to Matt. "Yes, Mr. Hornbeck mentioned to me that you'd be showing up here. I'm happy for the help. But tell me, Matt, what kind of experience do you have in building barns?"

"Not any." Matt shrugged.

Old Bob crossed his arms and looked Matt up and down. "Well, you're in luck then. You're just in time to take part in a barn building from the ground up. We're just getting in the foundation and starting to get the barn frame ready. I'm working on the sill timbers here. Say, why don't I take you around to meet the crew?"

Matt fell in step next to the carpenter, and as they walked Old Bob talked about the plans for the barn.

"As barns go, this will be a medium-sized one," Old Bob said. "It's what we barn builders call a four-bent barn. Each of the main frame sections is called a bent, and this barn will have four. We make up the bents on the ground, and then there'll be a barn raising to stand them up plumb and connect them together.

"But I'm getting ahead of myself," he said as they approached the low wall of bluestone that would be the new barn's foundation. "Let's start at the bottom. Matt, meet Asa—he's our stone mason."

Matt took one look at Asa and guessed he must be the strongest man he had ever seen. The mason worked shirtless, and Matt could see thick slabs of muscles moving under the sunburned skin of the man's shoulders. Asa's arms were all knotty and corded with muscles, and his stomach looked like Matt's grandmother's washboard. Watching all those muscles move made Matt think of the time his father had brought home a leather sack of squirming piglets.

"Pleased to meet you, Matt," the mason said and stuck his hand out. All the workmen Matt knew had calloused hands, but the skin of Asa's hands was as hard and gray as the stones he worked.

Asa was laying up the wall, guided by a taut string that marked the outline of the building and the eventual top of the foundation. As Old Bob and Asa chatted, Matt looked at the stonework and was impressed by how the corners of the foundation were sharp and square and the faces of the stone walls were even, with no wide gaps or projecting stones. Matt wondered how the mason had been able to piece together the irregular chunks of bluestone into such a regular surface.

Then Old Bob led Matt over to where another man worked, hunched over a short stout log. The man wielded a wooden, club-like maul in his right hand and a froe in his left. The froe was a tool shaped like an L, with a blade attached to a wooden handle. The maul reminded Matt of his grandmother's potato masher, only much bigger.

"Matt, this is Orrin, our shingle-maker," Old Bob said. "Orrin, meet Matt. He's joining our crew."

Orrin set down the maul, touched the brim of his hat in silent acknowledgment, and returned to his task. Matt watched as Orrin tapped the froe blade into the top of the log with the maul and twisted the handle back and forth to start a split. Orrin tapped the back of the blade again with the maul, then worked the froe down the length of the log, splitting the wood off in a thin, even shingle. The man worked fast and skillfully, and in the few minutes Old Bob and Matt watched, the man split off a dozen shingles.

"Orrin's a quiet one," Old Bob said as they walked off. "He spends his winters alone in a shanty, shaving barrel hoops, and never speaks to anyone the whole time. He's been doing that for most of his life, and I do believe he's plain forgotten how to talk."

From there, Old Bob led Matt to where three carpenters worked measuring and sawing the logs to be hewed into timbers for the barn frame. On the two ends of the long saw were Samuel and Benjamin—two grinning men in their twenties—while Harold, an older man with a pipe in his mouth and a pencil on his ear, did the measuring and marking. Near where the carpenters worked, Matt recognized piles of lumber he knew had been sawed at Mr. Keator's sawmill. The tobacco juice he saw staining a couple of the planks was a dead giveaway.

By the time Matt had met and talked to everyone, it was midday, and Old Bob and the crew knocked off for the noon meal. As they ate under the chestnut tree, Old Bob sketched the framing plan for the barn in the dirt with a stick and pointed out to Matt all the structural parts and their names. The carpenter explained how each part worked with the others: how the projecting tenons and notched mortises would fit together, how the corner braces would stiffen the whole structure, and how the hardwood pins would be driven to tie it all together.

Froe

Maul

"The key to making it rigid is these diagonal braces that create triangles in the frame. A rectangle can rack out of shape, but there's just one shape a triangle can take. It can't deform," Old Bob said.

As the carpenter explained the plans, he quoted from Pythagoras and Euclid, two of the famous Greek mathematicians whose names Matt had heard in school. The boy had seen plenty of barns in his life, but he had never appreciated before that barns were made of more than wood and stone. They also were made of these ancient mathematical principles men had figured out and turned to their use. A barn frame, Matt suddenly realized, was nothing less than a geometric figure—not one in a school-book, but one you could see and feel.

After they had eaten, Old Bob returned to work on the sill timbers, while Matt helped Orrin. There was a supply of short hemlock logs over by the wagon shed, and Matt loaded them into a wheelbarrow and brought them over to the shingle-maker. Orrin nodded or pointed at things he needed, but he never uttered a word. Old Bob was right; Orrin was so quiet he was spooky.

Toward the end of the day, Matt drifted back to where Old Bob was still working on the sills. Matt enjoyed watching the carpenter work. He liked the rough cut-and-slice texture left by the broadax and the neat rectangular mortises that the carpenter had chiseled into the sides of the sills. Old Bob said the mortises would match the tenons on the ends of the sleepers, which was the strange name he gave for the floor beams.

"Why do you suppose they call them sleepers?" Matt asked.

"I guess because when the barn's done, they'll be lying

there in the dark tucked in under the floor," the carpenter said with a smile and a wink.

That night after supper, Matt told his grandmother all about his day at the barn site and about Old Bob. His grandmother listened attentively as she washed fresh-picked strawberries in a basin at the sink. Emily was glad to see Matt's enthusiasm. He had seemed so quiet and moody lately. Even the camping trip to the hemlock woods had failed to cheer him up. She waited for Matt to finish and then revealed the surprising coincidence she had been holding back since the boy had started talking.

"I know Old Bob—but he was young Bob then. He and I were in school together when I was a girl," his grandmother said. "He was older than me and sat in the back of the room. When he got out of school, he went away and didn't come back here until about ten years ago to take care of his sister in Samsonville. She died about three years back."

"Where did Bob go for all those years?" Matt asked. The boy found he was curious about the carpenter.

"The way I heard it from his sister, he went to Massachusetts and became a ship's carpenter on a merchant ship out of New Bedford," his grandmother recalled. "He did that for twenty years, and it took him around the world. She showed me letters from England, Europe, South America, the islands of the Pacific Ocean—all over.

"After that, she said he was a master carpenter at a shipyard for another twenty years," Matt's grandmother continued. "Bob had a family out that way—a wife and three sons. His sons grew up and went to sea themselves. I heard one was lost when his ship went down in a gale.

Bob's wife died about twelve years ago—just before he came back here.

"For the last ten years, Bob's turned to barn building, which I guess is child's play compared to the complicated joinery that goes into building ships. You can learn a lot about carpentry from Old Bob, that's sure," Matt's grandmother said.

Matt tried to picture Old Bob as a young man on the pitching deck of a ship sailing foreign seas. The image put a faraway look in his eyes.

"I don't think I've ever met anyone who's been outside of Ulster County, much less all over the world," Matt said dreamily.

His grandmother turned from the strawberries with a sudden look of alarm on her face.

"Matthew Quick, I certainly hope you aren't thinking about going off to sea!" she said.

"No, no, Grandma. I'm staying right here," Matt said with a wide smile. "I've got a barn to build."

Chapter Eleven

Sills and Sleepers

Asa turned over the stone in his hand and studied it for a moment. With the narrow edge of his mason's hammer, he deftly tapped along a line that his eyes imagined on the stone. When he had scored the stone, Asa flipped it over in his hand and gave it a sharp rap on the underside. The stone broke along the line, and Asa dropped the piece into a gap in the wall.

Matt passed the mason another chunk of bluestone, and this one went uncut into a hole that Asa had waiting for it. The boy marveled again at the mason's ability to assemble this jigsaw puzzle of stones into the regular shape of a stone wall. When he asked the mason how he accomplished such a feat, the man scratched his bushy beard with thick fingers and frowned. Finally, his huge shoulders lifted in a shrug.

"I don't rightly know, Matt. It just seems that when I look at the stones, I don't see stones," Asa said. "I see a stone wall in pieces, and it's my job to put it together."

Asa turned back to his task. His eyes scanned the stones spread out around him. When he pointed out the stone he wanted next, Matt passed it to him. Matt had the impression that Asa already knew the order in which he would use all the stones at his feet.

With Matt bringing stones in a wheelbarrow to replenish the mason's supply, Asa's wall had reached the level of the taut string by midmorning. At last he slid the final

104

piece into place, gave
it a tap with his
hammer, and
stepped back to
inspect it. Asa
walked around
the whole foun-
dation of the barn,
looking over his work.

Beetle

"I think we have 'er
here, Bob," Asa called as
his eyes searched the wall
for imperfections. Old Bob
walked over and stood at Asa's shoulder. He
nodded his approval.

The men of the crew already had placed the big
main girder, which was a thick oak beam that spanned the
length of the barn in the middle of the foundation wall.
The girder was set into the stonework and was level with
the top of the foundation. Its function was to support the
sleepers in the middle so the barn floor wouldn't sag
under the weight of a loaded hay wagon.

Now it was time to place the sills. The crew leaned four
logs against the foundation to make an incline and then
rolled the sills to the foot of the incline. Using thick poles
as levers, the men slid the four sills up the incline one by
one. When they were in place atop the wall, Asa used a
huge wooden mallet called a beetle to tap the sills into
their final alignment.

After Old Bob sighted down the sills and pronounced
them level, the mason went around chinking any gaps he

found under the sill with thin pieces of stone. The mason also had the job of boring the holes for the pins in the overlapping sill joints at the corners (the men all said that when Asa put his big arm to the T-shaped auger, the wood couldn't get out of the way fast enough). Now it was time to fasten the sills with the pins. Ben, one of the young carpenters, mounted the sill carrying the beetle and a sack of hardwood pins he had whittled. The young man placed an oak pin in each of Asa's hole and drove it in with the beetle. As Ben walked the sills driving the pins, Matt could hear the heavy blows of the beetle echo back across the hills. Matt thought the barn's foundation and sills looked solid and substantial, and he was proud to have helped put it together.

"So, Matt, now that the sills are in place, what do you say we get to work on the sleepers?" Old Bob said. Matt followed the carpenter over to a row of logs that had been set aside for the sleepers.

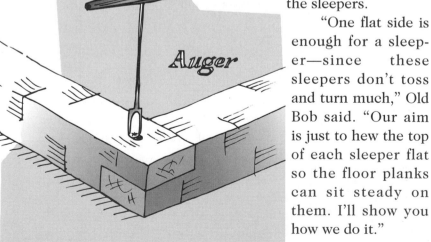

Auger

"One flat side is enough for a sleeper—since these sleepers don't toss and turn much," Old Bob said. "Our aim is just to hew the top of each sleeper flat so the floor planks can sit steady on them. I'll show you how we do it."

The carpenter picked up a dusty cloth sack and withdrew a chalk-coated string from it. He gave one end to Matt and showed him where to hold it at the end of the log. Then Old Bob walked to the other end of the log, stretched the string taut, and plucked it with his finger. The chalked string left behind a sharp, straight white line on the log. Old Bob and Matt repeated the operation on the opposite side of the log, creating a second line parallel to the first.

"Now if old Euclid was right, we just connect these parallel lines with some saw cuts, chop out the wood between the cuts, and we'll have us a nice neat plane surface for the top of our sleeper," Old Bob said.

The carpenter took the long-toothed handsaw and made a few saw cuts between the lines they had snapped, then he handed the saw to Matt.

"Here, Matt, you have a try," Old Bob said.

Matt went to work vigorously sawing at the log.

"Hold up now. Take your time and don't force the saw—that'll bind her up," Old Bob said. "Let the tool do the work at its own speed. Your arm just kind of goes along for the ride." The old carpenter moved Matt's arm in a slow easy rhythm to illustrate what he meant.

Matt relaxed into the easier rhythm of the sawing and before very long there was a neat row of parallel saw cuts spaced along the length of the log.

"Very good," Old Bob said. "Now how about trying your hand with the broad ax? The idea is to swing it real careful and split off the wood down to the chalk line we snapped. It's called hewing to the line. Here, watch how I do it."

As the carpenter talked, he worked over the end of the

log, showing Matt how to swing the ax in just the right shallow arc to carry away the wood without sinking the blade too deeply into the log.

After Old Bob had hewn a four-foot section of the log flat, he handed the broad ax to Matt. As its name suggested, the ax had a broad blade; Matt noticed that the blade was flatter on one side than on the other, and the ax handle curved gracefully off to the side. Old Bob explained that the flat side and curved handle was to help you swing the ax in a flat arc across the face of the log.

Matt hefted the broad ax, which had some weight to it. He began chopping out the wood between the saw cuts and found it difficult to swing the ax in just the right flat arc with any force. Soon, his arm began to feel tired.

"You're doing fine," Old Bob said. "Just try to concentrate on swinging the ax nice and regular and don't worry about how hard you hit with it. The force of the blow isn't as important as the control—it's the edge on the ax that does the job."

After a while, Matt began to get the knack of the ax work, too. Like the saw, it was a matter of rhythm and feel, not of strength. By late afternoon, Old Bob and Matt had hewn a half-dozen sleepers. Finally, Old Bob let Matt take the lead in measuring and snapping the chalk lines. It pleased the boy to contribute more than muscle to the job, and as the day grew late Matt looked with satisfaction down the row of sleepers they had made.

"Hey, we got the starch out of this job today," Old Bob said, clapping Matt on the shoulder. "Looks like I got me a real helper."

The workmen bantered back and forth as they turned from

their tasks
and gathered
up their tools.
Suddenly,
Samuel called
out to the others
in a low voice, "Look
alive, here comes
Farmer Hornbeck and his
missus."

chalk line

*Broad
Ax*

Samuel cocked his head toward
the opening in the stone fence where
Mr. and Mrs. Hornbeck could be seen
approaching. Mr. Hornbeck always made a
visit to the barn site at day's end, but Mrs. Hornbeck sel-
dom ventured past the rose bushes that lined the picket
fence at the house. It was odd to see her at the barn site—
and slightly ominous.

The farmer and his wife stopped about a hundred feet
off, and the crew could see Mrs. Hornbeck sweep a hand
across the spread of fields and then turn to shake her finger
in Mr. Hornbeck's face. The farmer had his hands outspread
and appeared to be trying to soothe the woman. At last, Mr.
Hornbeck nodded his head and approached the barn crew.

"Good evening, Mr. Hornbeck," Old Bob said.

The farmer stood quietly with his hands on his hips and
looked over the barn foundation. When he turned to face
Old Bob, his face wore a hesitant expression.

"Well, Bob, I see you have the foundation completed
and the sills in. Fine work, fine work," Mr. Hornbeck said.
The farmer shuffled his feet nervously.

"I—I suppose it's too late to face the barn another way, isn't it?" Mr. Hornbeck asked in a pained voice.

The men of the barn crew all looked at each other in amazement, but Old Bob responded to the question in a matter-of-fact tone.

"Why, yes, Mr. Hornbeck, that would be inconvenient at this point," Old Bob said, "but why would you want to do that?"

The embarrassed farmer frowned.

"It's the missus's notion, Bob," Hornbeck said in a low voice. The expression on the farmer's face seemed a plea for understanding and sympathy.

"See, that big wall of the barn will face due south. Mrs. Hornbeck says the wall of the garden shed up by the house faces due south, too. The siding on the south side of the shed got all warped by the sun, she says, and now wasps have taken to flying in the gaps under the warped siding and making nests," Mr. Hornbeck explained. "She's afraid that wall of the hay barn will become one big wasp's nest—so she wants it to face another way than south."

Old Bob scratched his gray head and looked at the men. And then he looked over toward Mrs. Hornbeck in the near distance. The farmer's wife stood with her arms folded across her chest. Most of her face was hidden in the shadow cast by the starched bonnet—but the men could all see the determined set of her mouth.

There was a moment of uncomfortable silence, until Matt cleared his throat and spoke.

"Just tell Mrs. Hornbeck that we'll cover the south side of the barn with quarter-sawed siding," he said.

All eyes turned toward the boy, as the men hung on his

next words. Matt cleared his throat and imitated Mr. Keator's best schoolmaster's tone.

"You see, if we side the barn up with quarter-sawed siding, the boards won't warp," Matt explained. "The grain's more even, so the boards dry evenly and there's no gaps—right, Bob?"

The old carpenter's face spread into a wide smile until his eyes had all but disappeared in the web of wrinkles. He forced his face into a serious expression, gave Matt a wink, and turned back to Farmer Hornbeck.

"Yes, yes, the boy's exactly right, Mr. Hornbeck," Old Bob said. "Wasps are a common problem in barns. Tell Mrs. Hornbeck she's wise to consider it.

"Of course, every good barn builder knows the remedy to wasps is quarter-sawed siding. It's fool-proof," he continued. "You tell that to Mrs. Hornbeck and tell her not to worry. Actually, we planned to put quarter-sawed siding on that wall all along ... Right, boys?"

The members of the barn crew nodded as one person and murmured their agreement.

"Splendid, splendid. So there's no need to move the barn, then," Mr. Hornbeck said.

Now the men all shook their heads together.

"Well, keep up the good work," the farmer said.

As Mr. Hornbeck strode off happily, the men in the barn crew rolled their eyes and turned their backs. Asa's huge shoulders heaved with a silent, suppressed laughter while the others coughed loudly to disguise their own mirth. Mrs. Hornbeck heard the strangled sounds and whirled away in disgust from what she thought was the sound of the workmen spitting. Mr. Hornbeck fell in behind her.

The crew could see him talking and gesturing with his hands as he hurried to keep up with his wife.

Old Bob chuckled as he looked after the departing couple. He put a hand on Matt's shoulder.

"We've built many a barn hereabouts, but this is the closest we've ever come to un-building one," Old Bob said. "Looks like you've saved the day, Matt."

The crew members laughed outright now, and they all clapped Matt on the back. Even Orrin made a sound that Matt took to be a word of praise, although he couldn't quite make it out.

Later, as Matt walked the long road home from Hornbeck's in the fading light, he rubbed his right arm. It was sore from the unfamiliar motions of sawing and hewing with the broad ax, but he felt better going home this night then he had felt in a long time. The work with Old Bob and the other men was so much better than the grunt work at the mill. The barn building took care, and know-how. At the close of each day you could see what you had produced, and gradually it added up to something at the end.

The boy smiled broadly to himself. It sure was better than endlessly shoveling sawdust and throwing scraps into piles that were never done!

Chapter Twelve

Posts and Beams

It was more than an hour past dawn, and the flock of crows complained loudly at the noise of Matt running down the narrow deer trail through the woods. A squirrel chattered in alarm, and another joined in. Matt could see one of them on the limb above the trail, his bushy tail twitching nervously.

Today, Matt was late. Clara had gotten loose and he had not been able to start off to work until he had chased her down and returned her to the fenced pasture. Matt was surprised at how fast the lumbering cow could run and how nimbly she could dodge him. After nearly an hour, he had gotten her cornered in the barnyard, where she had finally given up with a rebellious moo and a toss of her big head.

Now the boy was trying to make up for lost time. The woodland path was a shortcut he had found to Hornbeck's farm. The overland route through forest and fields cut a good mile off the walk down the road through Samsonville to the farm.

Matt was eager to get to work at the barn site. After three days of sawing and chopping, Matt, Old Bob and the crew had finished the sleepers. Old Bob had said that today they would begin to notch the posts, which were the upright timbers that were assembled with the horizontal beams to make up the barn bents. Matt didn't mind working with Asa on the bluestone wall and helping Orrin split the shingles. But hewing the sleepers with Old Bob whet his appetite for the more interesting carpentry jobs. Matt hoped that working on the posts and beams would let him practice the new skills he had been learning. He didn't want to miss anything by being late.

Matt breathed hard as he ran along the shady trail with his mind racing ahead of him, already on the barn building. He was jarred back to the present as he rounded a bend and startled a deer browsing on a bush at the edge of the path. Nostrils flaring, the frightened animal leaped over the trunk of a fallen tree and veered off the path into the woods. Matt, coming close behind, leaped the same fallen tree but kept to the path.

At last, Matt broke through the edge of trees at the bottom of Mr. Hornbeck's rolling hay fields. As he ran through the knee-deep grass, the boy could see Old Bob at the barn site already working over the row of hewed timbers. Matt dashed up and bent over with his hands on his knees, panting.

"Sorry ... late," Matt managed to gasp at last. "The cow ... loose and ..."

"Hold up there, Matt," Old Bob said. "Save your breath—what's left of it."

The carpenter sat down on one of the long, square-hewed timbers and waited for Matt to recover his wind. As he sat, the carpenter studied a sketch he had unrolled and spread out on his lap. Soon, Matt had caught his breath and stood looking at the sketch over Old Bob's shoulder as he pointed out where they would cut the mortises in the post.

"This is where we get to do some of the finer work," Old Bob said with a wink. "What do you say we get to it?"

Old Bob spread the sketch out on the ground so he could refer to it. Then, using a ruler, a carpenter's square, and a thick pencil, Old Bob measured and marked the location and shape of each of the mortises. He rechecked the accuracy of his marks against the sketch.

"Now's the time to make it fit," the carpenter said. "'Measure twice, cut once,' I always say.

"After we cut all the mortises and tenons, we'll temporarily assemble the bents on the ground to make sure the pieces all fit together tight and to mark the holes we need to bore for the pins," the carpenter continued. "Then, on the day of the barn raising, we'll pin each bent together permanently, stand them up one by one, and join them to each other."

Matt nodded. He already knew a little about barn raisings. There had been one at the Quick farm when he was about six years old. He remembered it as an exciting event with lots of people, children to play with, and good food. He even remembered the creaking of the heavy barn bents as they were pushed erect by the throng of men, and the excitement and shouting as they clambered up the bents to secure the cross braces. He had been so impressed by the power of people to do great things when they worked together. Most of all, he remembered the special pride he had felt when the frame was erect, the rafters were in place, and his father had climbed clear to the ridge to nail a small evergreen bough there for luck.

Old Bob worked skillfully with the square and pencil and soon had outlined the shapes of the several mortises required for the post. "Last evening, I chiseled out one of the mortises at the top of this post as an example for you," Old Bob said. "This particular mortise is for the tenon of one of the cross beams. Here, have a look."

Matt inspected the neat, rectangular hole cut into the post and wondered how Old Bob had achieved such a regular shape. As if in answer, the carpenter unrolled a leather bundle on the ground. The bundle contained a couple of odd-shaped chisels and another tool that looked like a thick-headed ax. Old Bob picked up the ax first.

"This is called a mortise ax, but you don't swing it—you hit it with a maul. It's really more like a chisel with a handle," Old Bob explained. "I use it for starting the cuts along the long edge of the mortise."

Old Bob set the tool aside and picked up a thick chisel with a wedge-shaped edge. It looked heavier than an ordinary wood chisel. "This here is the mortise chisel, which is used for

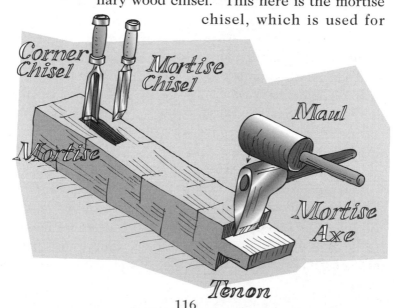

Corner Chisel

Mortise Chisel

Maul

Mortise

Mortise Axe

Tenon

clearing out the wood from the mortise," he said.

Then the carpenter picked up the oddest tool of the three, a chisel with a right angle bend in its edge. "I guess you can figure what this corner chisel is good for. It makes nice square inside edges for your mortise."

Old Bob placed the mortise ax along a side of one of the rectangles he had penciled on the post. Then he hefted the maul and struck the back of the mortise ax. After he had started the cuts this way, he switched to the mortise chisel to chip out the wood, and soon a smooth, square notch began to take shape in the post. As a finishing touch, Old Bob squared off the corners with the corner chisel.

"Here, Matt, you give it a try," Old Bob said, when he had brushed the last of the wood chips out of the finished mortise.

Matt picked up the mortise ax and placed it on the pencil marks that outlined another mortise. The boy hesitated.

"Do you put the ax inside the line or outside the line?" Matt asked.

"Right on the line, Matt. A good carpenter always erases his mark," Old Bob said.

Matt's tongue stuck out of the corner of his mouth in concentration as he positioned the mortise ax carefully and then struck the ax with the same sharp, even blows he had seen Old Bob use. After a while, on the carpenter's suggestion, the boy switched to the mortise chisel. Matt worked slowly and carefully. The wood split evenly under the blows and Matt smiled with pleasure as the empty square shape of a mortise begin to emerge from the side of the post. When he was finished, Matt could see his work lacked the near geometric perfection of Old Bob's mortise, but it was very definitely a workmanlike job.

"That's very good, Matt," Old Bob said enthusiastically. "I do believe you have a talent for this work."

Matt was pleased at the carpenter's words. The boy looked with pride at the mortise. Then he noticed some long cracks in the wood and asked the carpenter about them.

"They're called checks, Matt," the carpenter explained. "They don't affect the strength of the post. It's just where the grain of the wood has split some in drying. This timber has been drying for over a year waiting to be a barn post.

"That reminds me—I'm a little dry myself. While you start the next mortise, I'll go grab us a bucket of water from the well," the carpenter said. "You must be a little dry too after that long run."

Old Bob started off toward the well beyond the stone fence in the farmyard, as Matt turned his attention back to the post. He carefully placed the mortise ax on Old Bob's line and tapped on it with the maul to begin the first cuts on another mortise. Suddenly, Matt's concentration was broken by a rough but familiar voice from over his shoulder. Matt looked up and saw a dark shape blotting out the sun.

"Hey, schoolboy, I've seen kittens spanked harder than that," Tom sneered. "Here, let me show you how a man works."

Tom grabbed the mortise ax from Matt's hand and roughly shoved the boy aside. He seized the maul, raised it over his head, and brought it down with force, burying the mortise ax deep in the wood.

"That's how it's done, schoolboy," Tom said derisively. "I have to go back to the sawmill now, but I should be back this way tomorrow delivering another load of planks. I can pull that ax out for you then."

Tom laughed and walked away. He climbed up onto the wagon seat and started off in a commotion of hooves and creaking leather.

Matt eyes stung and his shoulders sagged as he watched Tom disappear through the gap in the stone fence. Inside, the boy felt that same coldness that he had felt the day of his dunking in the millpond. Then Matt was suddenly aware of Old Bob standing behind him, looking on. Beyond the carpenter, he saw Asa, Orrin, and the rest of the barn crew watching, too. The carpenter looked over at the mortise ax buried in the post and then turned his gaze to the boy. Old Bob didn't speak right away but looked at Matt thoughtfully.

"Tom thinks I'm not strong enough for a man's work," Matt said quietly. The boy looked at his feet, and then he raised his eyes to meet Old Bob's. "He's right, isn't he, Bob?"

"From what I just saw, Tom doesn't know much yet about being a man," Old Bob replied, "or about the work of making a decent mortise, either."

He smiled but his eyes had lost some of their warmth and glinted with something deeper.

"Animal strength is a gift from our Creator, Matt, and it's a fine gift. But it's not the measure of a man or of a man's work. You have your own gifts, Matt, and you'll discover them in due time. But when you do, remember: What's important about our gifts is the way we use them. It's our task to be worthy of our gifts, not prideful of them," Old Bob said. The carpenter stood quietly and looked at the boy.

"Now, let's get back to work, Matt," he said. "This barn isn't going to stand up by itself."

Matt was not consoled. Maybe Old Bob was right, but there was still the coldness that Matt recognized as fear. The boy smiled weakly and turned back to the mortise ax buried in the post. Matt worked the handle up and down like a pump until he could pull it free of the post.

"I have gifts, all right," the boy thought bitterly. "I have the gifts of weakness and fear. They know it at the sawmill, and now everybody in the barn crew knows it, too."

Chapter Thirteen

A Trip to Samsonville

The sounds of mauls and axes striking wood created an irregular rhythm, repeated by the echoes returning from the near hills. Farmer Hornbeck stood with his hands on his hips and a pleased look on his face and surveyed the scene at the site of his new hay barn.

The stringers were in and the barn deck was complete now. It looked like a big stage, waiting for the curtain to rise on the show. Around the deck, the finished timbers were lined up side by side, ready to take their places in the frame. At one end of the site, Harold directed Benjamin and Samuel as they temporarily assembled a bent on the ground and marked the places where holes for the pins still had to be bored with the auger.

The farmer rubbed his hands together in satisfaction. He looked around, spotted Old Bob, and hurried toward him.

"Bob, everything looks splendid. It's really coming along," he said enthusiastically. "I'd like to ask Reverend McHarlow to announce the day of the barn raising at church this week. How does the end of July sound to you?"

"Yes, everything should be ready by then," the carpenter said.

"Fine, fine, Bob." The farmer walked off, still rubbing his hands together, then stopped abruptly and came back.

"Say, I almost forgot. Bob, would you take the wagon into town today and see the blacksmith about the hardware we need for the barn door?" Mr. Hornbeck asked. "I'd do it myself, but something important has come up here and I can't get away."

"I'd be happy to, Mr. Hornbeck. I'll be off as soon as I check on a couple of things," Old Bob said, "and I'll take Matt with me."

Soon, Old Bob and Matt were up on the wagon and headed out Hornbeck's lane to the town road. As they passed by the white farmhouse, Matt noticed that most of the parlor furniture was out on the lawn. Then he saw Mr. Hornbeck and his hired man coming out of the house straining under the weight of a rolled-up carpet. Behind the men, Mrs. Hornbeck appeared in the doorway. Her starched bonnet bobbed up and down like a duck's bill as she vigorously swept a cloud of dust out the open doorway.

Old Bob nudged Matt with his elbow and winked, and they both smiled. The boy was glad for the chance to talk to the carpenter. Matt had so many questions about the work they were doing, but there wasn't always time to stop and ask them when they were in the midst of a task. Old Bob was an encyclopedia of information on his trade, and the best part was that Matt felt comfortable talking to the carpenter. As the wagon rolled on to Samsonville, the boy asked questions freely.

"Bob, why is it that the posts aren't thicker than they are? It seems to me the upright pieces should be a lot bigger, since they make the whole building stand up," Matt said. "Instead, we've made the beams bigger."

"That's because wood is stronger standing up than lying down—it's stronger bearing the weight with the grain, rather than across the grain like the beams do. After all, straight up is how the tree grows. That's the way the finished lumber is strongest, too," the carpenter explained.

Matt thought about Old Bob's explanation as the wagon creaked into Samsonville. It was midday and the hamlet was bustling with workmen, tanners, farmers, and farmers' wives coming and going. A few businessmen in coats and top hats could be seen on the streets, too.

"Bob, it still seems odd to me that the wood could be stronger one way than another," Matt said. "It's the same piece of wood no matter how you lay it down or stand it up."

"What we need is an illustration," Old Bob said.

Just then, the wagon rolled by Schoonmaker's Restaurant in time to see the door swing open and Louis Burkett stumble out onto the plank porch. Mr. Burkett was a local businessman whom everybody called "the Squire." The man had acquired a law degree in his youth but had never practiced law, living instead on the rents he collected on several farms his family owned. Still, Mr. Burkett always dressed formally, wore whatever elaborate sideburns and chin whiskers were in fashion, and signed every piece of correspondence with "Louis G. Burkett, Esquire"—even his instructions to the laundry woman. Over the years, the village wags had turned the Squire's law school title into a comic one.

As always, the Squire was decked out in a rumpled black coat, a top hat, and a black tie and carried a thin hickory cane with a brass horsehead handle. The man teetered unsteadily and shaded his eyes with a hand as he blinked in the sunshine. Then, reaching into an inside pocket of his coat, the Squire drew forth a pint bottle of a popular patent medicine called Dr. Sanford's Invigorator.

He unscrewed the cap, put the bottle to his lips, threw his head back, and took a long gulp.

The Squire was a large man—over 300 pounds, it was said—and he suffered from a number of chronic ailments, including gout and dropsy. No doubt he had downed many doses of the medicine already today. As the Squire stood on the porch feeling the effects of the hot sun and the alcohol-based concoction, he swayed like a sawed-off tree picking a direction to fall. All that held up the Squire was the thin hickory cane with the horse-head handle.

"Look, there's your proof," Old Bob said as he nodded toward the Squire leaning heavily on the hickory cane. "The Squire's cane. You could break that hickory cane over your knee, but end-on, with the grain, it'll support quite a lot of weight—as you can see."

Matt chuckled as the horse and wagon plodded past the restaurant and on to the blacksmith shop. Old Bob hopped down and went in alone with the sketches of the iron hinges Hornbeck needed for his barn door, while Matt took the opportunity to walk up the road and look around.

When he came to Tripp's General Store, the boy peered in the store window and then walked in for a look around. Matt found he had to wait for a minute for his eyes to adjust to the dark interior. The walls of Tripp's General Store were lined with high open shelves bearing everything imaginable: shoes, hats, kitchen ware, farm implements, oil lamps, brooms, flour, canned goods, bolts of fabric, tinware—the selection went on and on. Matt noticed a sign over the counter written in a flourishing hand: "If we don't have it, you don't need it—J. Tripp." Mr. Tripp himself stood under the sign, waiting on a woman with a basket hung over her arm.

As Matt scanned the shelves, he saw a section lined with bottles and boxes of patent medicines. He was curious about Dr. Sanford's Invigorator and took a bottle off the shelf to read the label. One by one, Matt began to read all the labels on the patent medicines. When he got to Carter's Spanish Mixture, he was amazed at the long list of physical problems the medicine claimed to cure. "Carter's Spanish Mixture," the label read, "is a Great Purifier of the Blood, with not a particle of mercury in it. Let the afflicted read and ponder. It is an infallible remedy for Scrofula, King's Evil, Rheumatism, Obstinate Cutaneous Eruptions, Pimples or Pustules on the Face, Blotches, Boils, Ague and Fever, Chronic Sore Eyes, Ringworm, Scald Head, Enlargement and Pain of the Bones and Joints, Stubborn Ulcers, Lumbago, Spinal Complaints and all Diseases arising from an Injudicious Use of Mercury, Imprudence in Life, or Impurity of the Blood."

Matt wondered what was left to cure after a dose of Carter's Spanish Mixture, but there were lots more bottles lining the shelves. As Matt read all the claims on the labels, he couldn't help wondering why the graveyards were so full.

Suddenly, Matt heard the sound of heavy footfalls. He turned toward the sound and there in the bright doorway was Tom's dark silhouette. Tom's eyes had not adjusted to the interior gloom and he had not seen Matt. Matt felt that coldness in his gut return, and he wedged himself in a corner behind a cluster of mops hanging on the wall.

Tom strode over to the counter where Mr. Tripp stood. The boy spoke to the proprietor and pointed at something in the store window. Mr. Tripp nodded and then walked to the front of the store, leaned into the window to retrieve the item, and brought it back to the counter. Matt couldn't see what it was because Tom blocked his view. Then the boy stepped aside and Matt saw a little girl's straw hat with a turned-up brim and a red ribbon.

"It's a real pretty hat, Tom," Mr. Tripp said. "It's the only one I have like it. Your sister Mary will love it."

"Yeah. It's her fifth birthday," Tom said with a wide smile. "Ma's making her a dress to go with it."

The boy dug in his pocket and produced a couple of crumpled bills and handed them to Mr. Tripp. The store owner accepted the money, returned some change, and then wrapped the hat in brown paper before he handed it to Tom.

"Wish Mary a happy birthday for me," Mr. Tripp said, smiling. Tom nodded and smiled back. He thanked the storekeeper and left.

Matt stood in the shadows, confused. There was that mystifying gentle side of Tom again. The coldness in Matt's middle had been replaced by a sense of shame, but he couldn't put his finger on just what it was that he was ashamed of. Was it that he was afraid of Tom? Or was it that he had failed to win the respect of the boy at the sawmill? Or both of those things? And Matt wondered why his own feelings of self respect were so wrapped up with Tom, anyway.

Matt realized that his grandmother was right—a person's reasons can be all muddled, but just knowing that doesn't always unmuddle them. Matt wished that one of the patent medicines that lined the shelves behind him could cure the confusion he felt in his heart.

Chapter Fourteen

Old Bob's Tale

As Matt and Old Bob headed back to the Hornbeck farm, the boy brooded in silence. The creaking of the wagon, the clip-clopping of hooves, and the buzzing of the flies around the horses' flicking ears were the only sounds as they rode along. The silence and Matt's glum expression told Old Bob that something was bothering Matt. The two had ridden for about five minutes when the carpenter finally spoke.

"You know, I don't live too far from here,"Old Bob said. "Suppose we take a side trip over to my place before we head back to Hornbeck's? There's something there I want to get."

Matt nodded but did not speak.

In a few more minutes, Old Bob turned the wagon down a side lane into the woods. The winding lane followed the bank of a small creek through a shady stand of hardwoods and at last emerged into a clearing, where a small, weathered house stood. Like Old Bob's clothes, the house lacked frills, but it was skillfully built, and it looked tight to the rain and cold. The nearby woodhouse was stacked full of firewood and the well-weeded vegetable garden was surrounded by a neat split rail fence.

Old Bob tugged on the reins, and the wagon rolled to a stop next to a set of rough slab wood steps. Matt and the carpenter hopped down from the wagon and climbed to the front door. Old Bob pulled the latch string, swung the door open, and Matt followed the carpenter into a single large room.

The first thing that caught Matt's eye was a large wood-carving mounted high up on the wall. The carving depicted a bosomy, unclothed woman from the waist up, with her streaming hair covering the places where modesty demanded. The carving was cracked and worn and showed traces of old paint, and it took Matt a moment to realize he was looking at the figurehead of a sailing ship. It was probably from one of the ships that Old Bob had sailed on around the world.

Now the boy looked around. Old Bob's house was part woodshop, part library, and part living space. Along one wall, there was a neat workbench with dozens of handsome chisels hanging over it, their well-honed edges gleaming. On the workbench, the boy also noticed a vice with a length of hickory clamped tightly in it. The hickory showed the marks of a drawknife, and there was a pile of wood shavings beneath it on the floor. Matt also saw a stone grinding wheel that worked with a foot pedal and, next to it, the rusty head of an old framing hatchet. There were many other tools too, including some that Matt did not recognize.

"What are all those odd-looking tools?" Matt asked.

"Those are my shipbuilding tools. I'm afraid they don't get much use anymore," Old Bob said. "But here, let me get what I came for."

Old Bob walked across the room and began to rummage in a high bookcase that held scores of leatherbound volumes. On the spines of the books, Matt saw the names of famous thinkers and writers he had heard about in school. There were the ancient Greeks that Old Bob had quoted—Euclid and Pythagoras—and others: Plato and Aristotle and someone called Heraclitus. There were books by Isaac Newton, whom Matt knew was an important mathematician, and by Voltaire. Matt knew he was famous too but couldn't remember why. And there were many strange names that Matt did not recognize at all.

"You sure have a lot of books," Matt said admiringly.

"Some of the sea cruises I went on took two years or better, and books are great company when time is heavy," Old Bob replied as he searched the shelves for the volume he wanted.

Matt knew what the carpenter meant. He had always thought of reading as being like a conversation between the author and the reader. The author's part was the words on paper and the reader's part was the new thoughts that the book sparked.

At last, Old Bob pulled a book from the shelf. He handed it to Matt.

"This is something you might want to read to help with some of your questions about the barn building," Old Bob said.

The book was *The Carpenter's Pocket Directory.* "Containing the best Methods of Framing Timber Buildings," the title page announced. The author was a man named William Pain, and it was published in 1797. As Matt leafed through the well-thumbed book, he saw drawings much like those Old Bob had sketched in the dirt.

Matt glanced up from the book at the old ship's figurehead and the rows of leatherbound books. The boy already respected Old Bob for his carpentry skills and knowledge, but now he had gained a new appreciation for the old man's experience and intellect as well. Matt suddenly realized that, in many ways, the old carpenter might be the most experienced and educated man he knew. The Reverend had book learning, but it was all in one thing. It was the same with General Samson, who was a knowledgeable businessman, and with Mr. Keator, who knew sawing inside and out, but little else. Old Bob had been around the world and had known a lot of different people and had read and thought about the words of history's greatest men. Most important, Matt felt easier talking to Old Bob than to just about anybody else. Maybe the carpenter could help him sort out some of the other questions that nagged him. It was worth a try. The boy swallowed and began.

"Bob, I want to ask you about some things that have been bothering me," Matt said, and he set the carpenter's book on the table. "It's not about barn building this time."

"Well, sit down then, and let's hear it," Old Bob said. He pulled out two chairs from the table and offered one to Matt.

Matt took the seat, drew a deep breath, and started talking. He told Old Bob about losing his parents and the sadness that wouldn't go away. He talked about the sawmill and Tom and about trying to come to terms with the older boy. He recounted his dunking at the millpond and how he thought he had lost the respect of the men. And finally he confessed to Old Bob the cold feeling inside and his sense of failure and shame. Matt left nothing out, and it felt good to get it all off his chest.

The old carpenter listened attentively, his hands folded in front of him. At last Matt had finished the story. Old

Bob continued to sit quietly for a moment, and then he spoke in a slow and deliberate voice.

"Well, Matt. I'm just an old carpenter, and I don't have a ready answer to all your questions. People are a lot more complicated than framing up barns," he began. "But I do believe that sometimes the rules of barn building carry over to other parts of life, too."

"You asked before about the barn posts, and I told you how wood was stronger with the grain rather than across the grain—like the Squire's cane," he said. "I believe that's true for men, too. Men have a grain to them, only we call it by another name. We call it 'character.' The strength of wood is in the grain; the strength of a man is in his character."

The carpenter waited to see if the boy understood what he was saying, and then he continued.

"When a man has good character, we call him 'upright,' like a barn post standing plumb, bearing its load with the grain," Old Bob said. "A man can be big or small, smart or stupid, but when we recognize strength of character there, we respect him for that—whatever other talents he may have or lack."

The carpenter's words aroused feelings the boy could not quite put into words, even in his own thoughts. He knew the old man was getting at something, but he was unsure just what. He looked questioningly at Old Bob.

"Anyone can see you have a fine heart, Matt. Now I think it's time to show you have grain, too," Old Bob said.

"How do I show my grain?" the perplexed boy asked.

Old Bob looked hard at Matt with his dark glinty eyes.

"The next time you feel that cold feeling inside, don't

let it drown out what your heart is saying," the carpenter said. "Listen to your heart and it will tell you how to show your grain."

Matt just stared at Old Bob. He was confused by this talk. He just wanted Old Bob to tell him something specific he could do.

"By 'showing my grain,' do you mean I have to stand up to Tom?" Matt asked.

"The fact is, Matt, Tom is not your problem. It's that cold feeling you've got to stand up to," Old Bob said.

Matt looked at the carpenter with a blank expression.

"Let me tell you a little story to illustrate what I mean," the old carpenter said. He leaned back in his chair and a faraway look came into his eyes.

"Many years ago, when I was at sea, there was a sailor on my ship who was afraid of gales. Storms are common at sea, and every time the wind kicked up, this young man would go all cold inside. Many times, as the wind howled, he'd take to his bunk and close his eyes tight and pray for deliverance," Old Bob said.

"The young man wanted to be a sailor more than anything, and he knew his fear must be conquered, but he didn't know how to do it," the carpenter continued. "He brooded about it for a long time. Finally, he went to the captain, who had many cruises under his belt, and told him about his problem.

"Well, the captain listened to the young sailor," Old Bob said, "and then he told the sailor that the next time there was a gale, he would be one of the sailors assigned to tend the helm. If he couldn't do it, he would be put off the ship at the next port."

"The sailor couldn't believe his ears because the helm was about the most dangerous place to be in a gale. It took two men to handle the ship's wheel in stormy weather, so strong was the force of the seas. What's more, the helm was on deck, exposed to the wind and the breaking waves. The helmsmen had to be lashed in place with ropes to keep them from being swept overboard," Old Bob said. "Just thinking about being on the helm in a gale made the sailor colder inside than he had ever felt."

"Of course the next gale wasn't long in coming, and it was a god-awful one. When the wind kicked up, the captain had the young sailor and the regular helmsman lashed fast to the two big wheels. The young sailor's innards were cold as ice water.

"When the storm broke, the wind howled, the waves grew into mountains, and the ship fell into the steep valleys between them, then bucked up the opposite slope. Wave after wave rolled down the deck and washed over the young sailor," Old Bob said.

The old man had a fierce look on his face now and, as he spoke, he gestured with a clenched fist. Matt sat in rapt attention, imagining the fury of a gale at sea and not blaming the sailor one bit for the fear he felt. There was a silence, as the carpenter seemed lost in the memory of that storm. At last, Old Bob resumed the story.

"For twelve hours, the gale held and the young sailor clung to the wheel and fought it," he said. "And when the gale finally had passed, they untied the two helmsmen, and the captain asked the young man if he had been scared."

"And that's when the sailor suddenly realized that the

cold feeling was gone," Old Bob said. "He had a stronger respect for the power of gales than ever before, but he didn't have that cold feeling of fear anymore."

Old Bob looked hard at Matt.

"The sailor didn't beat the gale, Matt. No man can beat a gale. But we can beat our fear by standing up to it, " Old Bob said. "That sailor showed his grain when he got off his bunk and stood up on deck and faced his fear square."

Matt was concentrating hard on the carpenter's words, turning them over and over in his mind.

"Remember what we said before—if the Squire put his weight across the grain of his cane lying flat, it would break like a toothpick," Old Bob said. "But upright, the grain in that thin stick of hickory can stand up to his weight and a lot more."

Matt did not say anything. He was thinking about Old Bob's story. It put things in a new light, but he would have to think about it some more. Then, almost as an afterthought, a question occurred to him.

"What ever happened to that sailor, Bob? Did he get to stay aboard?" Matt asked.

"He became the best ship's carpenter to ever sail out of New Bedford," Old Bob said. The carpenter smiled and winked at the boy. Matt responded with a wide grin of his own.

"I guess it's time to get back to Hornbeck's farm," Old Bob said. "Mr. Hornbeck will be about through cleaning house by now, and he'll be wandering out to the barn site to pass on his missus's instructions."

As they rode back in the wagon, Matt looked at the framing book in his lap, but his thoughts were elsewhere.

Old Bob was in a quiet mood, too, and neither spoke again until they had arrived back at the barn site. As Matt climbed down from the wagon, Samuel trotted over, waving a piece of paper in his hand.

"Here, Matt. Ned was out from Keator's sawmill delivering another load of planks, and he left this note for you," Samuel said.

Matt took the scrap of paper from Samuel's hand and read in Mr. Keator's familiar scrawl, "Matt, we need you back at the mill. I'll see you there tomorrow. George Keator."

Matt passed the note to Old Bob and heaved a deep sigh. The carpenter read the note.

"That's all right, Matt. The crew and I will be finishing up the timbers in the next few weeks. Then the barn raising should come along pretty soon after that," Old Bob said. "We'll see you again then."

Matt attempted a smile, but his heart wasn't in it. He was already looking ahead to his return to the flitch pile and the sawdust and Tom.

Chapter Fifteen

A Tussle with Tom

Matt marched up the hill to Mr. Keator's sawmill with a willing step, although his teeth clenched a little when he came within earshot of the whining saw. As the boy walked through the mill-yard, he saw that the pile of logs had dwindled considerably since he had been to the mill last, but to his dismay he saw also that pile of sawing scraps had grown much larger. Working alone, Tom had fallen behind.

"Well, hello," Mr. Keator called out as the boy approached. The sawyer worked the lever to stop the spinning saw, and he and Basil and Ned all came over and greeted Matt warmly. Tom stood off from the group, working at the scrap pile. He had his back to the others as he shouldered a load of the wood slabs.

After greeting the sawmill crew, Matt walked over and shouldered a load too.

"Good morning, Tom," Matt ventured pleasantly as he walked past the bigger boy returning from dropping his wood. Tom grunted a greeting but kept his head bent over as he walked.

As the two boys toted the scraps, Matt found to his surprise that he could almost keep up with Tom now. The weeks of hard outdoor labor had hardened the growing boy's muscles. Although the work seemed easier, it was no less boring, especially compared to the carpentry work alongside Old Bob.

It didn't take long for Matt to fall back into the rhythm of the sawmill work, and during the morning break, while Mr. Keator sharpened the saw, Matt made his rounds greasing the machinery, just as before. As the crew rested, he told them about Mrs. Hornbeck and the wasp's nest incident. Basil slapped his knee and the pipe in his mouth bobbed up and down as he laughed. Mr. Keator liked the story, too, because now Mr. Hornbeck would be increasing the cost of his order with the more expensive quarter-sawed boards.

"I wonder if I can get Mrs. Hornbeck over to all the barn building sites around here," Mr. Keator chuckled. "It sure would be good for business." They all laughed and Matt thought he even saw Tom grin.

After the break, Mr. Keator said the boys would have to make a bonfire to get rid of the huge pile of slabs and scraps. Mr. Keator hated to have a fire in the yard because of the danger to the mill, but the pile had gotten too big and had to be disposed of. The boys worked hard hauling the scraps for the rest of the morning, and by afternoon they had made a pile as big as a haystack at a spot a hundred feet away from the mill buildings, which Mr. Keator judged was safe enough.

Matt threw a match into some wood shavings at the edge of the pile and in no time the sappy hemlocks were blazing twenty feet into the air. As the day wore on, Matt and Tom made trip after trip, feeding wood scraps into the roaring fire. It was hot work on a hot day, and the boys took off their shirts. Soon, their bodies were wet with sweat and smeared with soot and sap. By the late afternoon, the bonfire had dwindled to a heap of embers and smoking ash, and the scrap pile in the millyard was much reduced. The boys sat sweating in the shade.

"Hey, boys, I bet a dip in the millpond would feel good," Mr. Keator said with a broad smile. "How about it?"

Matt and Tom took one look at each other and grinned. In a moment more, the boys had stripped off their clothes and run shouting into the millpond. Matt whooped as he dove into the cold water. Then he opened his eyes in the cool and peaceful world of rippling light beneath the surface of the millpond. Matt stayed under the water for a few moments, trailing bubbles from his mouth and watching the little trout dart into their lairs under the overhanging banks.

He surfaced for air and floated on his back, looking up at the lush green treetops sweeping the sky. He could see Tom out of the corner of his eye, floating in the pond and squirting water into the air with his mouth. Maybe working at the sawmill wouldn't be so bad after all, Matt thought.

The day passed and then another, as the whining saw spit out board after board, most of them headed for Hornbeck's new barn. Usually, Hornbeck's hired man came to pick up the lumber, but once Matt surprised the barn crew by showing up with a load himself. He was excited to see how well the work was coming along. Most of the framing timbers were done now, and as Matt and Old Bob walked around, the boy pointed out and named the barn parts he recognized. Matt had been reading the carpenter's old barn framing book in the evenings and had learned a lot. Old Bob was pleased. The visit had been enjoyable, and Matt went back to the sawmill reluctantly.

It was Matt's fourth day back at the sawmill, and the mill

crew sat in the shade eating their noon meal. Mr. Keator suddenly hurried up, holding a piece of paper in his hand and wearing a distracted look on his face.

"Say, boys, I got this note from Mr. Hornbeck with his lumber order, but I left my spectacles down at the house and can't make it out. How about one of you boys deciphering it for me?" Mr. Keator asked. Tom happened to be closest to the sawyer, so Mr. Keator handed the note to him. He spit tobacco juice into the sawdust and looked at the boy expectantly.

Tom held up the paper in his hands and stared at it blankly. A long second passed and the boy's shoulders seemed to sag as though a heavy weight had settled on him, a weight even his brawn could not lift. Matt saw Tom's predicament, and without a second thought he reached over and snatched the note away from the older boy.

"Here, let me see it, Tom. Hornbeck's chicken scratching is a little tough to make out," said Matt.

The boy skimmed the note and grinned, then read it aloud: "It says, 'Dear Mr. Keator. Please take notice that I won't pay for any more lumber with tobacco juice on it like that last load had. Mrs. Hornbeck says it's disgusting.'"

Basil and Ned burst into laughter as Mr. Keator's face reddened. The sawyer harrumphed indignantly, snatched back the note, and stalked away grumbling. Ned and Basil—still chuckling—drifted back to work too, leaving Matt and Tom standing alone. Suddenly, Tom turned to Matt and spoke to him through gritted teeth, his eyes blazing.

"I guess you think you really showed me up that time, don't you, schoolboy," Tom said angrily. "Well, I'm tired of you putting on airs. Now you'll be getting yours."

The boy began to move toward Matt with a clenched fist, and Matt felt that familiar coldness rush into his midsection like a winter chill coming in an open door. He fought an urge to run and only backed up a step.

"No, Tom, you got it all wrong. I was just trying to help you—to cover for you before the men realized you couldn't read that letter," Matt said. He struggled to keep his voice calm and not betray the fear he felt.

"You're lying, Matt. You think I'm a fool just like the rest of them at school did. Just like people thought my father was. I'll show you who's the fool," Tom said.

The larger boy continued to come toward him, and still Matt backed up. His mind raced as the cold filled his insides, and he remembered what Old Bob had said about showing his grain. Matt knew he could not beat Tom in a fight. He wasn't big enough, and fighting was not in his nature anyway. But Matt could stand up to the bigger boy and speak the truth. Yes! That could be the way to show his grain!

But first he had to beat the coldness—that's what Old Bob had said. Matt struggled to swim to the surface of the coldness that flooded him, just as he had swum to the surface of the millpond. At last he broke the surface, took a deep breath, and looked straight into Tom's eyes. Matt spoke quickly and hoped the boy would see his words were true.

"I know you can beat me, Tom, but you can't make me scared of you no more," Matt blurted. "I know some things about you. You want to be tough all the time, but I know you're not. I know you wear an apron sometimes and hang clothes on the line. I know you're kind inside and that you love your mother and your sister Mary, and I know that you miss your dead sister and your father."

Tom narrowed his eyes and continued to walk toward Matt, but there was something else in his eyes besides the anger. Matt kept his eyes locked on those of the larger boy and spoke again.

"I know how you feel, Tom. I know because we've both lost people we loved," Matt said. The boy paused to let the words sink in—just as he had seen Mr. Keator do.

Tom looked uncertain. His hands were no longer balled into fists; they hung at his side and clenched and unclenched nervously. Now Matt spoke in a softer voice.

"I think maybe we're a lot alike, Tom," Matt said. "We need to help each other, not fight with each other."

Tom had stopped coming forward and stood there with his hands hanging at his sides. Matt's unexpected words had aroused new, confusing thoughts in Tom and the angry fire in his eyes had subsided. Matt had stopped backing up and now faced his adversary squarely.

"Tom, I know about how you wanted to go to school, and I thought it was unfair the way the schoolmaster and some of the kids at school treated you," he said. "And I know that when you left school, it was to help support your mother and sister, not because you were lazy or stupid."

Tom still had not spoken. His lips were pressed tightly together and he wore a look of indecision. Matt guessed that, inside, Tom was struggling to see things in a new way. He decided to tell Tom one more thing.

"Heck, Tom, I can teach you to read, too, if that's what's bothering you," Matt said with a grin. "There's no reason you can't learn to read just because your father couldn't."

All at once, the anger flared back into Tom's eyes as Matt's words touched a nerve. Tom rushed the few feet that separated him from Matt and grabbed the boy by his shirt front. The worn and much-mended fabric tore as Tom thrust his face into Matt's own.

"If there's any lessons to be taught here, I'll be teaching them, schoolboy!" Tom sputtered.

Tom drew his arm back and threw a punch that grazed Matt's nose as he struggled to tear free. Unable to break the bigger boy's grip, Matt threw his arms around Tom's middle and hugged him tight, just like he was clinging to a tree trunk. Tom could not direct a punch at Matt in that position, so now he was the one trying to break free. The two boys grunted and spun around like awkward dancers. Matt held on. As their feet tangled, both boys fell to the ground. Matt could feel Tom's greater strength threatening to break his grip, but he locked his hands together behind Tom's back and hung on tight as they rolled and grunted in a cloud of sawdust.

Then Matt heard shouts and, in a few moments, felt rough hands on him as the other men dragged them apart. Matt's shirt hung from his shoulders in tatters, his nose felt sore, and he could taste blood, but when he searched for the feeling of coldness in his stomach, it was gone.

Tom, panting from the tussle, stood off to the side and glared at Matt, while Mr. Keator stood between them and turned his head to shoot angry looks at first one, then the other. Mr. Keator was working his tobacco plug harder than Matt had ever seen before. The sawyer reared back and spit so hard the bolt of tobacco juice raised a plume of dust when it hit the ground.

"What in blazes has gotten into the two of you?" Mr. Keator ranted. "You boys act like cats and dogs—and rabid ones at that! Well, I'm fed up with you both! I'm not paying you wages so you two can take licks at each other! I should whip you both myself! And as for you, Tom ..."

Matt turned and walked off down the lane. Behind him he could hear Mr. Keator still laying into Tom. Matt had walked all the way to Samsonville Road and crossed the bridge before the yelling at the sawmill finally was drowned out by the rushing water of Mettacahonts Creek.

Chapter Sixteen

A Gift from Old Bob

The muscles at the top of Asa's shoulders bulged as round as cannon balls, as his arms made powerful circles with the auger handle. When the auger bit into the timber, the wood squirmed out of the hole like a coiling, pale worm.

Matt and Old Bob stood side by side and looked on while Asa bored the hole in the post for the hardwood pin. After he had bored through the post and withdrawn the auger, Samuel and Benjamin joined the beam to the post and tapped the joint together with the beetle, and then Asa stuck a pencil in the new hole and marked the beam. They pried the joint apart again, and Asa placed the auger on the beam to make the hole that would align with the hole he had just bored in the post—only Asa seemed to be boring just a little off the mark. Old Bob pointed at the auger tip.

"What's Asa doing wrong, Matt?" the carpenter whispered out of the corner of his mouth to the boy.

"Nothing, Bob. He's supposed to bore the second hole a little off. That way, when the pin is driven, it'll pull the beam up tight against the post," Matt whispered back.

"Right you are, Matt," Old Bob said with a wink. "I thought I might trip you up on that one."

Matt had been back at Hornbeck's barn site working with Old Bob for more than a week now. After Matt had gone home with his shirt all torn up, his grandmother had been ready to go down to the sawmill and raise cain with Mr. Keator, but Matt had been able to talk her into going to see Old Bob instead. Now, thanks to the carpenter, Matt was back working full-time with the barn crew.

The barn site looked far different than it had on that day in June when Matt had driven Mr. Keator's wagon through the gap in the stone fence. The timbers for the barn bents were nearly finished, and the daily wagon loads of lumber from the sawmill had added up to stack upon stack of lumber. Orrin's shingle-making had produce quite a pile as well. You could still hear the blows of the maul against the froe, but the shingle-maker himself was hidden behind the rising heaps of shingles around him.

Matt was glad to be back at the carpentry work, and he had thrown himself into it with enthusiasm. The boy had finished reading the framing book and had borrowed other carpentry books from Old Bob, too. Matt was glad the days were long now, because he could read late without having to use up a candle. After each evening's reading, Matt made it a point to try to use the lesson the following day at the barn site. He was learning fast with Old Bob as a teacher.

Old Bob was impressed with Matt's rapid progress, too, and soon he was entrusting the boy with more important tasks. Old Bob left it to Matt to measure and lay out the plates, which was what they called the timbers that joined the bents to each other at the top—just as the sill timbers joined them at the bottom. Matt worked carefully, then checked and rechecked his measurements. He was pleased when Old Bob looked over the work and pronounced it correct.

"Well, all we need are the roof rafters now, Matt," Old Bob said. "My question to you is, how do we lay out those rafters without having made the plates they sit on yet?"

"The sills at the bottom take up the same space as the plates do at the top," Matt replied. "We can just lay out the rafters on the sills."

"Well, I give up then, Matt," the carpenter said with a laugh. "If I ever hope to stump you, I guess I'd better stop giving you books to read."

By late July, the preparations for the barn raising had neared completion and all that was left was to whittle the hardwood pins. The barn raising date was only days away, and Matt and the others in the barn crew felt a rising sense of excitement.

On the Thursday before the Saturday barn raising, Mr. Hornbeck called the crew together for a little celebration. Mrs. Hornbeck had set out a table of huckleberry pies and coffee for the occasion, and the aroma started Matt's mouth watering. Mrs. Hornbeck's pies were known far and wide as prizewinners, and the men looked forward to their feast with eager anticipation. But before the refreshments could be served, Mr. Hornbeck stood upon a barn timber to commemorate the occasion with appropriate remarks. He raised a hand and when he had everyone's attention, the farmer cleared his throat and launched into a speech thanking the barn crew for their fine work. In school, Mr. Hornbeck had been a student of elocution and it still showed.

"Friends—and I believe I can call you friends—on behalf of Mrs. Hornbeck and myself I would like to thank you for the splendid work you have done on our hay barn over these recent months. It is heartening in this day of increasing indolence and sloth to see men who ..."

Mr. Hornbeck droned on for a full half hour, paying tribute to the crew's industry and skill and many other fine qualities Matt had not noticed. The men missed much of the farmer's speech because they kept being distracted by the smell of the steaming pies and coffee waiting on the table. At last, Mrs. Hornbeck cleared her throat loudly, and Mr. Hornbeck brought his speech to a halt in mid-sentence.

"... But I digress," Mr. Hornbeck said. "Let me simply conclude by inviting you to partake of our humble fare and ..."

The words triggered a rush to the pies, and Mr. Hornbeck had to shout over the clatter of silverware to tell the men that he was also giving them the next day off. There was a round of applause and whoops, and the men, their mouths watering, turned back to the table where Mrs. Hornbeck was serving up the slices of pie and pouring the coffee herself. The woman smiled in delight as each man in turn took a bite of her pie and pronounced it the best he had ever tasted.

Matt and Old Bob took their plates and sat under the chestnut tree, eating and talking about the barn raising. When they had finished their pie, Old Bob excused himself for a moment and went to fetch the canvas sack he always brought to work. He set it down before him and then called to the rest of the barn crew to gather around. When they had settled down on the grass, Old Bob rummaged in the sack and pulled out a wooden box.

"Listen up, boys. I had wanted to congratulate you all

on the fine work you did here, but I do believe that Mr. Hornbeck has used up all the words on the subject," Old Bob began with a smile. The men laughed, but Old Bob raised his hand to regain their attention. "So instead of that speech, I'll make another. Now, Matt here is new to our trade, as you know, but I think you'll all agree that no master carpenter has more enthusiasm than he does. If the boy develops half as much skill as he has spirit, he'll outshine us all."

There was a ripple of applause, and Old Bob's hand went up again.

"But there's one barn builder's necessity our boy Matt lacks. Fortunately, it is my pleasure to remedy that today," Old Bob said with ceremony. "Matt, I believe I speak for us all in presenting you with this gift as a token of our respect and esteem."

With that, the carpenter handed Matt the wooden box.

"Open it, Matt. Open it," several voices said at once.

Matt accepted the box and looked around at all the smiling faces. The boy lifted the lid. Inside, he saw a framing hatchet fitted with a handcrafted leather case. The boy's mouth fell open as he lifted the hatchet out of the box, took off the leather case, and hefted the tool in his hand. The blade gleamed and the hickory handle had been rubbed with oil until it was smooth and lustrous. The framing hatchet felt weighty and important in the boy's hand. Suddenly Matt recognized the tool.

"Bob, is this the old framing hatchet I saw at your cottage?" Matt said. "It looks like new!"

"I cleaned it up some and whittled a new hickory handle for it, is all," Old Bob said modestly.

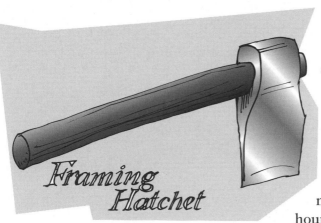

Framing
Hatchet

It was a profound understatement, Matt thought, as he recalled the rusty tool he had seen on the carpenter's workbench. It must have taken hours to restore the hatchet. It was beautiful.

"Turn it over," Old Bob said.

The boy turned over the hatchet and was thrilled to see that his own given name was carved in the hickory handle in clean, beveled roman letters as neat as any on a courthouse cornerstone: MATTHEW.

"Th-thank you, Bob," Matt stammered in surprise and gratitude. "Thank you very much. I'll take good care of it. I'll keep it sharp."

"I know you will, Matt. And next time I need a helper, I can call on one with his own tools," Old Bob said. The carpenter laughed and clapped Matt on the back. Then he turned to the other men in the barn crew.

"Well, boys, have yourselves a good day off tomorrow, but remember to be back here fit on Saturday," Old Bob said. "Never mind what Mr. Hornbeck said before, all we've made so far are piles of sawdust and wood chips. Come Saturday, we make the barn."

Chapter Seventeen

The Barn Raising

The day of the barn raising finally arrived, and the air was sultry and still even as the red sun cleared the Shawangunk Ridge. Matt stood in the doorway of the cottage listening to the buzz of insects and looked out toward Samsonville Road, where a series of wagons laden with people, tools, and baskets of food already had begun to rattle past on their way to Hornbeck's farm.

Matt had never felt so excited in his life. As he and his grandmother set off in their own wagon at the first light, the boy rankled at how slowly Lucy walked. He considered for a moment jumping down from the wagon seat and taking his shortcut on the run, but he didn't want to leave his grandmother, so he stifled the urge. As they rode along, he impatiently fingered the new framing hatchet that hung on his belt.

When they arrived at the barn site, Matt joined the other early arrivals who were standing around drinking coffee dipped out of a big iron pot over a low fire. The men passed the time talking in low voices as they squinted into the low rays of the rising sun and shook the cobwebs out of their heads.

Soon, scores more people had arrived. Matt saw Basil, Ned, and Mr. Keator from the sawmill. There was Bertram, too, and many other men from the tannery, including General Samson himself, who looked just like any other workman with his shirt sleeves rolled up and his thick forearms crossed over his chest. The Reverend McHarlow was there too, surrounded by the women from the church. Matt spotted Mr. Tripp from the store, and he even saw the Squire duck behind a big chestnut tree for the day's first nip of Dr. Sanford's Invigorator.

"Well, today's the day, boys, and it looks like we've picked ourselves a hot one," Old Bob said as he gathered his crew together. "When we get a few more men here, I want you boys to get together four teams and begin to make up the bents. Asa, you and Orrin take one team; Ben and Samuel, you take another; Harold, you get a team; and my partner Matt and I will get the fourth."

Soon the crew had organized the several teams, and, after some instruction, the men to begin to move the heavy timbers into position and assemble the bents on the ground. Old Bob saw to the work of his own crew, with Matt helping out, and then went from group to group checking the work on the other bents.

As the men worked, the women and children were busy too, setting up long plank tables with every kind of food and drink. There were loaves of thick bread, cheeses, and jar upon jar of fruit. There were more vats of coffee and somebody had mixed up a batch of switzel, a summertime drink made with water, molasses, ginger, and vinegar. Near the tables, a fat pig roasted on a rough spit over the coals of a pit fire, and, off to the side, several women worked plucking the feathers from a half dozen old roosters—soon to be roasters—who had crowed their last dawn.

Everyone was doing their part, and there was a festive spirit in the air. A barn raising was as much a social occasion as it was a community work project. Matt saw his grandmother and Mrs. Pierce laughing with the other women as they worked, and the children, excited by this unusual event, ran shouting in all directions. Matt saw Tom's little sister Mary wearing her new straw hat with the red ribbon on it. The girl was playing tag, and she laughed merrily as she ran from a little boy in blue overalls.

The feeling of excitement built as the work progressed, and by midmorning the men were moving the first of the heavy bents into place for raising. They were already wet with sweat from the heavy work in the hot sun.

It won't be long now, Matt thought, as he watched Samuel begin to pass out the long iron-tipped pikes to all the men. Then the boy noticed Old Bob talking to Mr. Hornbeck. The carpenter looked concerned about something, and Matt moved closer to overhear what he was saying.

"I don't like the looks of that thundercloud building over toward Sundown, Mr. Hornbeck. The weather's really boiling up," Old Bob said. He was pointing to the west, where a tall, dark thunderhead loomed. Matt noticed that the wind was kicking up too, and the trees were showing the undersides of their leaves—a sure sign of a coming storm.

Hornbeck squinted at the thunderhead and frowned. "It may blow by us, Bob. Even if it doesn't, I think there's time to get the first bent up. Then everybody can duck into the wagon shed until it blows over," Hornbeck said. "Blast the weather, I really need to get framed up today while everybody is here."

"Let's get to it, then," Old Bob said.

Old Bob gave a holler and beckoned to his barn crew and their teams of men. In a minute, the men had all grouped around the carpenter. Old Bob issued some last instructions and then clapped his hands. There were shouts all around among the men as they took their positions. A murmur of anticipation swept through the women and children as everyone stopped what they were doing to watch the first bent go up.

Old Bob shouted through cupped hands, and the gangs of men positioned themselves in ranks around the first bent. Matt, pike in hand, took his position just outside the first rank of men. According to the plan, the men in the first rank would lift the timbers shoulder-high, and hold them. Then Matt and the second rank of pike-wielding men would take the load on the tips of their short pikes and, on command, they all would continue the lift. A third rank of men with longer pikes would come in as soon as the bent had risen high enough, and, finally, when the bent was three-quarters of the way up, ropes could brought into play from the opposite side.

Old Bob looked around to make sure that everyone was in his place. There wasn't a sound. The women had stopped talking, and even the children had hushed. Everyone had their eyes fixed on the carpenter. Everything was ready.

"Get set!" Old Bob commanded and raised his arm above his head.

For a moment, the men all looked at each other, as though sharing a common thought leading to a common will. Then Old Bob gave the count: "One, two, three ... heave, boys!"

Old Bob brought his arm down sharply and, as one, the men in the first rank hefted the heavy timbers chest high with a chorus of grunts.

"Hold her, boys!" Old Bob called and the men braced the load on their chests. Matt sprang forward, dug the iron tip into the hewn upright beam, put his shoulder into it, and waited for the next count. It wasn't long in coming.

"To the top this time, boys! One, two, three ... heave!" Old Bob commanded.

Again the timbers creaked as the bent rose. Now all the men were lifting, and there were so many pikes they looked like the lances of a Roman legion. Matt was surprised at how easily the bent rose before the strength of so many. Then the ropes from the other side tightened and the weight diminished as the bent approached the upright position. In less than a minute, the first bent stood swaying slightly under the taut ropes, silhouetted against a dark, boiling sky. The men and women all gave a loud cheer.

Suddenly, a clap of thunder drowned out the shouts and the wind gusted fiercely. The treetops lashed each other, and Old Bob had to yell to be heard. "You there, Tom, nail a couple of braces on this bent real quick and then head for the wagon shed!"

Tom, who had drawn the job of bracing, had already nailed one end of the diagonal brace to the sill and was standing on a ladder to nail the other end of the brace to the upright post. Tom drove the nails into the brace with savage blows of his hammer, then raced around to the other side of the bent to secure the second brace.

Matt, his framing hatchet in his hand, hung back to watch Tom as the rest of the men followed the women and children to the shelter of Hornbeck's wagon shed. Matt saw Tom drive home the last nail and, with a final heavy blow, split the wood of the brace. Tom looked at the damaged brace and hesitated. Then, as lightning flashed nearby, he turned and headed for the shed. Matt could feel the concussion of the immediate thunderclap.

"The first brace is enough to hold it," Tom muttered as he ran by.

Matt fell in behind Tom. The main part of the thunderstorm seemed to be passing by to the north, but the boys still faced a fierce, gusting wind as they jogged toward the sheltering wagon shed. Scarves, papers, and shingles blew by them, and then a straw hat with a red ribbon whirled past in the wind. Matt could hear the hubbub in the wagon shed as the women tried to calm the children, who squealed in excitement and mild fear. "Now settle down, children," someone's mother said. Then Matt heard another voice above the noise. It was Mrs. Pierce.

"Where's Mary gone?" Matt heard the woman ask.

There were murmurs of uncertainty, and then someone pointed at the barn site and shouted, "There she is—at the barn!"

All heads turned to follow the pointing finger. There was Mary, her yellow curls whipped by the wind, bending over to pick up her straw hat from where it had blown up against the newly raised barn timbers. As the little girl brushed against Tom's first brace, Matt was stunned to see the brace fall away! In his haste, Tom had driven three nails into a wide check in the post and had missed hitting good wood completely! Now only the one damaged brace kept those heavy timbers upright.

The wind kicked up again. It tore Mary's hat from her hand and sent it twisting across the barn deck. Matt saw the upright barn timbers rack from the force of the wind, and there was the sound of wood cracking. Now the heavy timbers began to sway over Mary's head. Everyone was shouting Mary's name at once, but the desperate voices were lost in the howling wind. The little girl was intent on retrieving her new straw hat and was heedless of the danger over her head.

Matt had stopped midway to the wagon shed and was closest to the barn and to Mary. He turned and began to run toward the little girl as fast as he could. Behind him, he could hear shouts and the footfalls of others running, and his ears picked out Tom's anguished voice before it was drowned out by another fierce gust of wind. There was the renewed sound of cracking wood and a series of loud pops as wood fibers gave way.

Mere seconds had passed, but time seemed to have become slow and dreamlike. As Matt ran on feet of molasses, the barn bent shuddered against a final onslaught of the wind. Matt saw the damaged brace split in two and fall away, and, as if in a dream, the heavy timbers began to topple slowly. He saw the girl, buffeted by the gusting wind, slip on the wood planking and fall, still clutching her precious straw hat, and he saw Tom running at his side in slow motion, his face a mask of horror. The boy had his arms upraised as if to catch the timbers closing down on his sister like the jaws of a bear trap.

It was all happening so slowly, but Matt knew that neither Tom nor he could ever reach the girl in time to pull her out no matter how slow time became. In a rush of coldness, a feeling of fear and helplessness came over Matt, but he forced it out. He must save Mary—but how?

As Matt raced the falling timbers, he could hear behind him confused shouts of horror and helplessness. Then a voice seemed to cut through the rest. The voice was faint but clear—clear enough to be the boy's own thought. Was it a thought? Matt wasn't sure, but, voice or thought, the two odd words planted inside Matt's head burst into flame like a pine knot in the fire. Matt felt the weight of his framing hatchet in his hand and knew what he must do!

The barn bent had fallen halfway through its arc, and Matt was just a few feet away from the barn deck—he must act now! Holding the framing hatchet just under the head and thrusting it in front of him, Matt dove headlong toward the barn deck where the helpless little girl lay. In that swollen moment of time, the boy felt like a cloud drifting lazily above the earth.

The screams of the women and shouts of the men were drowned out by the crash as the falling timbers at last reached the barn deck. Then there was a lull as time seemed to stop altogether, and in that frozen instant between heartbeats, the hushed crowd saw Matt's framing hatchet jammed upright between the toppled timbers and the barn deck. The hickory handle had been split from end to end by the impact of the falling timbers, but its dense grain had refused to be crushed, and in the thin sliver of space the handle protected, lay Mary, her straw hat in hand. The little girl looked up and saw the blood-drained faces of the people in the crowd. Mary gave her first scream of fear, and time resumed.

Immediately, Mary's cries were overwhelmed by the crowd's cheers. Matt saw Mary's mother gather the crying girl in her arms, and he felt the hands of the men lift him to his feet and pound him on the back. Through the knot of people around him, Matt's grandmother suddenly appeared.

"Oh, Matt. You could have been killed," she said, and she hugged him tightly as tears streamed down her face.

Off to the side, Matt saw other men helping Tom up from the ground. One of Tom's arms hung strangely, and his face was contorted by a mix of pain and joy. When their eyes met, Matt saw other confused emotions crowd into Tom's expression.

Then Mr. Keator broke in. He grabbed Matt by the hand and pumped it vigorously. "Matthew Quick, you've given 'quick thinking' a new meaning around here! Your ma and pa would be god-awful proud of you. I know I am," the sawyer said. There was a noisy assent from the crowd and more slaps on his back.

Then Matt felt a hand laid on his shoulder and turned to look into the face of Old Bob. The carpenter's dark eyes shone brightly from within a web of wrinkles. "You've discovered your gifts, Matt. You have wit and courage, and no man was ever more worthy."

Matt basked in the carpenter's smile and then suddenly felt himself lifted clear off the ground. He was on Asa's big shoulders, and the stonemason was turning in a merry circle to the cheers of the crowd. Matt saw the joyous upturned faces of the people spin by below, and the boy felt something inside him loosen and begin to flow, like the ice washing out of the creeks in the spring.

Matt knew everything would be all right.

Chapter Eighteen

A Summer Afternoon

It was late summer now, and Hornbeck's new barn was filling up with hay, just as work was slowing down at the sawmill. The millpond was low and most all the logs were sawed up. Mr. Keator crouched at the idle saw, filing vigorously and chewing his plug of tobacco. He turned his head and spat tobacco juice into the sawdust, narrowly missing a pair of small feet in buckled shoes. The sawyer looked up to see a smiling face gazing at him from under a mop of curly blonde hair.

"Where's Tom?" the inquisitive face asked.

"He's over under the chestnut tree, Mary," the sawyer said and resumed filing the blade. The girl looked over to the spot where Matt and Tom sat in the shade. Tom's right arm was in a sling, and Matt held open a book as Tom traced a path across the page with his left index finger. Mary saw her brother smiling and talking excitedly to Matt about something in the book.

"Thank you, Mr. Keator," the girl said.

"Never you mind ...," Mr. Keator began—but as he looked at Mary, he raked a knuckle across a gleaming sawtooth. A trickle of blood appeared and began to spread down the back of Mr. Keator's hand.

The sawyer yelped and made a move to put the wounded knuckle in his mouth but then remembered the plug of tobacco there. A blasphemous oath rose in Mr. Keator's throat—but it stuck there when he saw Mary looking at him wide-eyed.

"Oh ... the *Squire's cane!*" Mr. Keator finally blurted, borrowing the odd oath he had heard Old Bob shout out in the midst of the uproar on the day the barn bent toppled. Mary looked worried at the sight of the sawyer's pained expression and touched his sleeve.

"It's not bad, Mary. Just a scratch. You get along now," Mr. Keator said.

The sawyer reached into his back pocket for the rag and wrapped it around the wounded knuckle. He watched as Mary skipped off through the sawdust and the happy sight swept away the pain. The sawyer smiled to himself and let go with another bolt of tobacco juice that hit the saw.

Mr. Keator looked at the brown stain oozing down his precious saw and frowned. The sawyer spit his tobacco plug onto the ground, looked at the soggy brown lump, and kicked sawdust over it in disgust. Then he took the rag from his knuckle and wiped the saw until it was shining again. The sawyer flicked the saw with his fingertip and smiled as the steel rang with a sweet, clear tone like a distant church bell.

The story of Matthew Quick is fictional, but the setting of the story uses many true facts about the Catskill Mountains and life in the mid-1800s.

The hamlet of Samsonville is a real place in Ulster County, New York. Although Samsonville's former glory is hard to see today, there really was a tannery there, described as "the largest tannery in America" in an article in the *Kingston Democratic Journal* on August 15, 1855. All that's left of the tannery now are some crumbling stone foundations.

No description of the specific tanning process used at the Samsonville tannery survives to the present day, so the tanning process and the work of the tannery's bark peelers in this story are based on accounts of practices that were then commonly in use in the Catskill Mountains. Bertram's report of the production and employment figures for the Samsonville tannery are drawn from actual historical sources, though.

There also was a sawmill and millpond upstream from the tannery in 1858, according to records and maps of the time. In fact, you can still see the ruins of a sawmill at the spot today, although the ruins appear to be those of a sawmill built later than the one described in this story.

Tripp's General Store, Schoonmaker's Restaurant, and Markle's Hotel were all actual businesses in Samsonville in the mid-1800s, too. They are gone today without a trace. Palentown Cemetery really exists where the story says it does, but there are no graves for Cyrus and Sarah Pierce or John, Catherine, and Noah Quick. Farther down the road, the Palentown School still stands, officially designated as a historic landmark. It is unused now, except at election time, when it becomes a polling place for citizens to vote.

As for the people in the story, they are all fictitious except one (I'll tell you who in a minute). But some of the names in the book are borrowed from real people. Quick, Keator, Hornbeck, Terwilliger, and Schoonmaker are all family names that date back to the first Dutch settlers in the Catskill Mountain region in the 1600s. Many people with those old Dutch names live in the Catskill Mountains to this day.

The real person from history? If you guessed General Henry A. Samson, you were right. General Samson really did own the Samsonville tannery, and the description of him in the story closely follows a description published in a newspaper account of the day. General Samson even spoke at the militia parade in the hamlet, just as the story says.

Many of the background events in the story are true, too. The Catskills were hit hard by a drought in 1854, and the account of the burning peat bogs is a true one. A cholera epidemic in the Rondout area (part of present-day Kingston) did occur in 1855, and cholera outbreaks were always a threat in those days. Dr. Sanford's Invigorator and the rest of the patent medicines in Mr. Tripp's store are all real examples of over-the-counter medicines of the mid-1800s. Their unbelievable claims are taken from actual newspaper advertisements.

Last, the descriptions of Old Bob's carpentry tools and crafts are drawn from the recollections of oldtimers, from the many fine books on the subject, and from visits to excellent museums, among them the Farmer's Museum in Cooperstown, New York; the Eric Sloane Museum in Cornwall, Connecticut; and Old Sturbridge Village, in Sturbridge, Massachusetts. I recommend that you visit them if you are interested in learning more about rural American life of the last century.

As for Matthew Quick—well, a boy by that name may never have lived the life I have imagined for him, but you can be sure that some boy like Matt lived a life very much like this story.

About the Author

Jeff Muise is a writer, public relations specialist, and former newspaper reporter who has had a lifelong affection for the Catskill Mountains and an interest in the region's folkways and history. Jeff, his wife Deborah, and their daughters Amanda and Molly live on a mountainside in Shady, New York, in an old farmhouse that Jeff renovated using carpentry skills he learned from his father. There, they tap their maple trees each spring, pick berries in the summer, and, in the fall, get whatever apples the squirrels miss.

If you would like to purchase another copy of *Old Bob's Gift* and you cannot find it in your local bookstore, please send a check or money order for $12.95 (plus $3.00 shipping and handling charge for the first book, and $.75 for each additional book—New York State residents add sales tax) to:

The Shawangunk Press
8 Laurel Park
Wappingers Falls, NY 12590